ELSEWHERE

Also by Alexis Schaitkin

Saint X

ELSEWHERE

Alexis Schaitkin

CELADON
BOOKS

NEW YORK

ELSEWHERE. Copyright © 2022 by Alexis Schaitkin. All rights reserved. Printed in the United States of America. For information, address Celadon Books, a division of Macmillan Publishers, 120 Broadway, New York, NY 10271.

Designed by Michelle McMillian

www.celadonbooks.com

Library of Congress Cataloging-in-Publication Data

Names: Schaitkin, Alexis, 1985– author.
Title: Elsewhere / Alexis Schaitkin.
Description: First edition. | New York : Celadon Books, 2022.
Identifiers: LCCN 2022004544 | ISBN 9781250219633 (hardcover) |
    ISBN 9781250219619 (ebook)
Subjects: LCGFT: Novels.
Classification: LCC PS3619.C32534 E47 2022 | DDC 813/.6—dc23/eng/20220207
LC record available at https://lccn.loc.gov/2022004544

Our books may be purchased in bulk for promotional, educational, or business use. Please contact your local bookseller or the Macmillan Corporate and Premium Sales Department at 1-800-221-7945, extension 5442, or by email at MacmillanSpecialMarkets@macmillan.com.

First Edition: 2022

10 9 8 7 6 5 4 3 2 1

For Emerson and Johanna

I

W e lived high above the rest of the world. Our town sat in the narrow aperture between mountains, the mountains forested, the forests impenetrable. A cool, damp place: ferns pushing up between rocks, moss on roofs, spiderwebs spanning the eaves, their strands beaded with water. Every day at dusk the clouds appeared, gathering out of nothing and thickening until they covered us with their beautiful, sinister white. They settled into everything, wrapped around chimneys and hovered over streets and slid among trees in the forest. Our braids grew damp and heavy with them. If we forgot to take our washing off the line in time, it became soaked all over again. We retreated to our houses, flung open our windows and invited the clouds in; when we breathed in they filled us, and when we breathed out they caught us: our dreams, our memories, our secrets.

We didn't know who cleared the forest and established our town, or how long ago. We could only guess at our origins by their traces, which suggested that whoever built this place had come from far away. Our streets and park and river carried names in a language we did not speak. An earthen embankment stretched along the river to protect us from floods, but this was unnecessary here. It never rained enough for a flood; we received only gentle showers of predictable duration. Our houses and shops featured steeply pitched roofs built for snow, though it didn't snow here. We had no seasons; our climate was always temperate and pleasant. What brought them to such an isolated location? Was there a time when people lived here as they lived elsewhere? Or was this place afflicted already, and did the affliction draw them here?

I find it difficult to determine when, as children, we came into an awareness of the ways our affliction set us apart. Even when we were too young to understand it, it showed up in our games and make-believe. Young boys could often be seen at the edge of the forest, huddled around piles of sticks and leaves and paper, holding stolen matches to the tinder until it caught and watching it burn. Young girls concealed themselves, crouching among the foxgloves in dooryard gardens, burying themselves under heavy quilts in their parents' beds, playing at being gone. Ana and I played 'mothers' constantly. We fed our dolls bits of moss and lichen and swaddled them in scraps of muslin. We crept to the edge of the skinfruit grove and stole fruits off the ground, rubbed the red pulp on our dolls' cheeks for fevers and healed them with our special 'tinctures,' river water from the Graubach. Our mothers were a pairing and Ana and I had been inseparable since we were born. We lived right across from each other on Eschen, one of our town's short backstreets. Our bedroom windows faced each other, and she was the first person I saw when I woke up and the last person I saw before I went to sleep. We would stand at our windows and press our hands to the panes, and I could swear I felt her hand against mine, like we had the power to collapse the distance between us. We used to tell people we were twins, one of those obvious lies small children tell; everyone in town knew us, knew our mothers, besides which we could not have looked less alike. Ana was the tallest girl in our year, everything about her solid: her legs strong and quick, braids thick as climbing ropes, big blunt eyes that stared at whatever they pleased. I was scrawny enough to wear her hand-me-downs, my braids so puny they curled outward like string beans, eyes cast up, down, away, never settling anywhere too long.

My doll was Walina and Ana's was Kitty. Such dirty things. We wiped our noses in their matted hair. We filched dried skinfruit vines from our mothers' piles and wove thorned cradles that scratched their limbs. We slipped our silver hairpins from our braids and used the sharp points to prick each other, then pressed the blood to our dolls' cloth torsos to give them pox. Once, we licked what remained of the blood off one another's skin, giggling nervously because we were doing something we shouldn't. We were supposed to keep the points of our pins clean, held fast in our braids, until we were grown and ready to prick a man's skin. Ana's blood left a hot tang in my mouth I tasted for days.

Often, we abandoned our dolls in the grass overnight. When we fetched them in the morning they were soaked, heavy as real babies. They stayed damp for days. We pressed our faces to them and breathed in their thrilling stink, like the wet pelts of goats in the forest. Sometimes we lifted our shirts and pressed our nipples into their rosebud mouths, and I imagined sweet, blood-warm milk flowing from me into Walina. We cared for our dolls wretchedly, but we loved them. I wondered later whether we had sensed that our mothers would go, and if this was what compelled us to treat our dolls as we did; or whether, somehow, it was our mistreatment of them that summoned the affliction to our mothers.

When Ana and I were out and about in town, we tried to watch the mothers like the grown-ups watched them and like the mothers watched each other, but we didn't really know what we were supposed to be looking for. We saw them alone and in their threes. At the Op Shop, we watched them try on dresses and slide gold hooks through the holes in their ears, studied them studying themselves in the mirrors. We pressed our noses to the windows of the dining room at the Alpina during afternoon tea, saw their hands bring the hotel's blue china teacups to their mouths, their lips move with silent gossip and speculation between sips. We lurked at the edge of the skinfruit grove when they gathered the fruits in their baskets and pulled down the spent vines. Sometimes a mother split one of the black fruits open and ate it right there, sucking out the red membrane and cracking the white teardrop seeds with her teeth. The mothers said the fruit was like nothing else. I tried to imagine it, but I couldn't; my mind doubled back on itself when it tried to think up a taste it had never tasted. We saw the mothers on their porches, snapping the thorns from the vines and weaving their baskets. We saw how they swayed with their babies in their arms, side to side like metronomes holding time for a song only they could hear. Sometimes a mother caught us staring. Ana would thrust out her tongue at her, and a feeling would come over me like the mother saw through me to everything I could not yet imagine I would do.

It was Ana who taught me to eat dirt on the mornings after a mother went. We did it when everyone gathered on the lawn. There was so much happening then, with the proceedings getting underway, so it was easy to slip off unnoticed. The rest of town was deserted on those mornings. We had it all to ourselves. We ate soil from pots of dancing lady on porch steps. We pulled grass from the playing fields at Feldpark and licked the dirt that clung to the white roots. In the forest, we coated our tongues with the dirt that hid beneath the slick black leaves on the ground. Ana never explained why we did this and I never asked. I was always content to go along with her schemes. When I ate the dirt, I imagined a forest growing inside me, every leaf on every tree the same as our forest. We were binding ourselves to this place, I understood that much. But I didn't know whether Ana saw our little habit as preventative, or whether she hoped in swallowing the earth to make something dark take root inside her, to feed it and make it grow.

Aside from 'mothers,' the only game we played with any regularity was 'stranger.' We had never seen a stranger ourselves, so naturally we found them fertile ground for make-believe. The last person to stumble upon our town from elsewhere had come before we were born, and nobody ever talked about her. True, we had Mr. Phillips, but that wasn't the same. He had been our town's supplier our whole lives, bringing goods to us four times a year; he came from elsewhere, but he wasn't a stranger.

We played in the forest, taking turns with who got to be the stranger and who got to be herself, coming upon them. We each had our own approach to playing the stranger. I imagined them wretched and cowed. I smudged dirt on my cheeks and pulled my hair out of the tight braids my mother must have woven. I moved erratically, darting this way and that, froze like a stunned deer at every snap of a twig underfoot, as if terrified by my own presence. When Ana came upon me I reached out to her and whispered, 'Help me. Help me.'

Ana's version was violent. She thrashed through the forest, eyes feral as the eyes of the goats. She bared her teeth at me and drew her hands into claws and made to scratch me, and I tried to make my mind forget that it was Ana, who I had never not known, and sometimes I got close, I saw only her wildness and the emptiness behind it, and I imagined that, having seen a stranger, I would never be the same.

It makes sense that we approached it so differently, because we had only the most elementary understanding of strangers. We knew only that the ones who had come to town in the past had all turned out to be disappointments, painful lessons in what life elsewhere made people into. Their lives were ruled by a simpler, thinner calculus. They sought only obvious pleasures and the avoidance of pain, and they would do anything to achieve these ends. They couldn't help it. They didn't have our affliction so they could not learn what it taught us, did not possess what it gave us.

But when a stranger did come, she was nothing like either Ana or I had imagined. This was at the end of upper year, when I was sixteen. By then, Ana and I had not been a pairing for a long time. She had severed our tie suddenly and brutally after our mothers went. From then on the memory of our friendship lived inside me like a potent dream, difficult to believe it had ever been real.

The stranger arrived in the afternoon, when I was working my shift at Rapid Ready Photo. It was my father's store. He took the formal portraits for everyone in town: school, wedding, newborn. He spent most of his days in the darkroom in the back of the shop and I worked the register after school. Like the other shops, we were never busy; we lacked the population to be. I spent my shifts doodling in the margins of my notebooks instead of doing homework. I practiced violin. I took coins from the register and bought fruit candies from the crank vend at the front of the store, let them lodge in my back teeth and worked over the rough sugar with my tongue. I spun myself slowly around on my stool, trying to match the speed of my revolutions to that of the fan overhead and watched the shop swirl around me. This is what I was doing that day when a blur out the shop's front window caught my eye. I slowed to a stop, looked out and there she was, way down Hauptstrasse, coming up the sidewalk. In our girlhood games, Ana and I had imagined strangers as extreme figures. But this woman appeared almost ordinary. Still, I could tell straightaway, when she was still quite far off, that she wasn't one of us. It was the way she carried herself, a difference in bearing, subtle yet profound. She held herself very erect, yet this had the effect of making her appear not haughty but guarded, vulnerable, like a small bird puffing itself up. She wore a dark crepe dress with small white flowers and soft brown boots on her feet. On her head, a straw hat with a band of black ribbon. She hadn't bothered to tie the ribbon under her chin; it flowed down her back against her hair. She carried a leather valise, which she let knock against her side as she made her way up the street, peering in the shop-windows. A camera hung from a strap around her neck, so I should not have been as surprised as I was when she reached our shop and stepped inside.

She approached the counter with her eyes downcast. When she reached it, she stood straight and still before me, though even in stillness a twitchy energy escaped her. I waited for her to speak, but for an uncomfortable amount of time she didn't, she just kept her eyes on the floor. I wondered if shops worked differently elsewhere.

'Can I help you?' I asked gently.

She looked up. We stood there, so close together, and stared at each other. When I had imagined coming upon a stranger as a child, it was seeing them that mattered, and letting their strangeness operate upon me. Yet it turned out what mattered most in that first encounter wasn't seeing her but being seen by her, a person who didn't know me. Beneath her gaze I felt my self sweep cleanly away, like flotsam borne off on the Graubach. Briefly, ecstatically, I wasn't *me* at all, but anyone and no one.

She looked at me with a sort of labored smile, like she was trying hard to show she wasn't hostile, or maybe like she feared I might be hostile. It was my first lesson in the stranger, that her every action, down to her tiniest movements, would suggest two opposed interpretations.

'A roll of film, please.' She spoke in the softest voice, like her throat was too clenched to let any more sound escape.

'So what brings you to our town?' I asked with an encouraging warmth as I fetched the film from a hook on the wall. It seemed she hadn't yet determined what kind of place this was, and I wanted to reassure her she had nothing to fear here. But my question seemed to have the opposite effect. A frightened look came over her, like her life had primed her to hear even a simple, friendly question as an intrusion, maybe even a dangerous one.

'Holiday,' she said unconvincingly. She had a habit, I was coming to notice, of stroking the black ribbon that hung down from her hat as if it were a creature she was trying to soothe. She must have been riding the train and seen our supply road winding into the mountains and decided to hop off between stations. I wondered what had happened to her elsewhere for her to end up here all alone and in such a state, although perhaps it was usual for a woman to be so skittish and agitated there.

As I rang up her film, she surveyed the shop.

'If you need something you don't see here, we can always put in a special order with Mr. Phillips,' I said. 'That is, if you'll be staying awhile.' I hoped she would tell me how long she planned to be with us, information I was desperate for personally and which would make me in-demand at school the next day. But it was like she hadn't even heard that part of what I said.

'Mr. Phillips?' she asked.

'Our supplier. He can get you anything. You just tell him what you need and when he comes back he'll have it. You'd like Mr. Phillips. He's a consummate professional.' I cringed at myself, parroting something I'd heard adults say. It was true though. He performed his duties with diligence and discretion, bringing our supplies and taking the baskets our mothers wove back to the city, where he sold them without telling anyone where they came from. We trusted him not to speak of us elsewhere. He didn't pry into our lives, nor did he burden us with his troubles. We knew it must be painful for him, the glimpses he got each supply of the beauty of this place and the force of our lives here, but he didn't let this show. He had been our supplier since the previous supplier, another Mr. Phillips, stopped coming when my father was a boy. He was so buttoned up about his work that we didn't even know whether the prior Mr. Phillips had retired or passed away, or whether our current Mr. Phillips was that Mr. Phillips's son, or if the name was merely a coincidence, or if this Mr. Phillips had taken the name of the other. According to the adults in town, the prior Mr. Phillips had been a different sort, frantic and addled, always rushing, his papers in shambles, and he often got orders wrong, or tossed our baskets into the freight car in so slapdash a way that some were inevitably damaged and rendered unsalable. Though some of the oldest adults said he hadn't always been that way, had in his prime been nearly as adept as our current Mr. Phillips, his suits pressed instead of rumpled, hair hard and glossy, not the gray tumbleweed it became. This was how life elsewhere worked upon people. They accumulated years rather purposelessly, so that as they aged they did not unearth their deepest, truest selves but, on the contrary, grew increasingly dispossessed of themselves.

The stranger laughed, amused by what I'd said about Mr. Phillips being a 'consummate professional.' I blushed.

'Are you alone here?' she asked.

'My father's in the darkroom.'

'Just the two of you?'

I nodded, and blushed again. It was my first time ever talking to someone who didn't know our situation, and it was embarrassing, even a bit painful, to have to confirm it. It was unusual for a father not to marry again after a mother went, and it was looked down upon. Ana's father had remarried in less than a year, and he and his new wife had three more children. But the stranger didn't know any of this, and to my relief she just smiled in response, at once piercing and vague.

When I told her how much it was for the film, she opened the valise, removed a change purse, and stacked the coins on the counter. I froze for a moment when she did that, but I quickly pulled myself together. I didn't want to make her self-conscious. I used one hand to sweep the stack off the edge of the counter into my other hand and sorted the coins into the register.

'Well, thank you,' she said.

'See you around. I'm Vera, by the way.' I said it as casually as I could manage.

'And I'm Ruth. See you around, Vera.'

For the rest of my shift I heard the echo of her strange voice saying my name, *Vera, Vera, Vera*, until it seemed a foreign, inscrutable thing.

In the coming days, when I told people about my first sighting of the stranger, it was the coins I returned to, how she stacked them on the counter like that. It was such a clear example of the tiny actions that betrayed so much about her and the place from which she had come. In our town, whenever money changed hands, we touched, fingertips brushing briefly as the coins passed from one hand to another. We didn't only do this with money. We touched whenever we gave or took something, when we shared a sip of our tea with a friend, or picked up a baby's fallen sock on the sidewalk and returned it to his mother. Even Ana, who was so often cruel to me, would never just set her coins on the counter when she made a purchase at Rapid; we let our fingers brush, a touch absent of personal rancor because it wasn't personal, it was communal, hundreds of small touches threaded through our days like the unconscious way you touch your own body. The stranger had never had this and she didn't even know she hadn't.

That night as we ladled stew into bowls, brushed the tiny pearl teeth of children and sang them lullabies, we felt the stranger's presence; it seemed we did these things for her, as if, while our town's population had increased by a single person, we had also doubled, become both ourselves and the sight of ourselves, now that we had a stranger to see us.

Once our children were asleep, the lovemaking began, bodies pressed together under heavy damp quilts. Husbands and wives were together that night not like people who had never not known each other, but with the passion and hunger of strangers. A husband saw not his wife with the pink scar their son liked to stroke and call *mama's worm*, felt not the fingertips callused by her instrument, smelled not the frying oil in her hair, talc on her thighs, but a mystery. The unknown of her rose above him, the precious things he knew of her reduced to almost nothing.

• • •

The atmosphere in town the next day was festive, everybody eagerly sharing news of the stranger. Sally made sure we all knew she'd been the first to see her. Sally ran the concession kiosk at the entrance to Feldpark, selling tea and shortbread and griddled sandwiches, and from that vantage point she had a clear view of the supply road's final steep stretch. She claimed the stranger told her she had never seen a more beautiful place. While we were happy to hear this, we did not want to ascribe too much significance to Sally's report. She was a shallow and unserious person, prone to embellishment, and she loved nothing so much as to be an authority on a subject of collective interest. We teenage girls often walked away giggling after we made our purchases from her. She was old enough that her hair was silver, and we couldn't get over the fussy way she styled herself, in lacy blouses and ruffled skirts, or her hair, which she wore in ringlets like a birthday girl. The boys our age loved to get Sally going, to draw out her most ridiculous behavior, which was easy to do. Once, Di, Marie, and I were behind Nicolas in line, and we heard him tell Sally her shortbread was the best in town, even better than his mother's. He leaned across the counter and whispered, 'Let's keep that our little secret, okay, Sally?' Like clockwork, she fluttered her eyelashes and tucked an extra short-bread into his waxed paper packet, and as she passed it to him and their fingertips brushed, she whispered, 'Our secret.' In fairness, it wasn't just us teenagers; Sally was one of the few childless women in town, and the mothers were always chattering about the way she badgered them with questions and pounced on the tiniest scraps of gossip about their lives, desperate to matter any way she could.

In the caf at lunch that day, everybody was talking about their first sightings. I told Di and Marie how the stranger had set her coins on the counter. Di, Marie, and I had been a threesome for years. I had secured myself to them shortly after Ana ended our pairing. We made for a somewhat unnatural threesome, frivolous Di and rigid Marie and quiet Vera, though like all threesomes we did everything together. Di told Marie and me she'd noticed the stranger wore no jewelry whatsoever in her hair. Marie recounted her sighting with particular relish. She had been practicing her cello by the parlor window when she looked up from her music and saw the stranger passing on the sidewalk. At first, she thought she was the woman from the framed illustration on the wall of the ice cream parlor. 'Isn't it funny, the tricks our minds play?' Marie said. It turned out Marie was in good company. Many of us mistook the woman, at first, for someone whose image we had seen before, in a painting or on the packaging for some product or other.

Stories began to circulate among us uppers of the most memorable sightings. Jonathan had come quite close to her. He had gone out to skin and clean the rabbit his mother would cook for supper. He had slaughtered it the day before and was lifting it from the basin of salt water, now dark pink, on the front porch when she walked past. He said the skin on her arms was all gooseflesh; she must have been so accustomed to the sweltering lowland heat that her body didn't know what to make of our refreshing climate.

Liese said that outside of her house on Gartenstrasse, the stranger had paused to smell the mother-of-the-evening that grew along the fence line. It was the end of the day, when the clouds were beginning to gather and the flowers released their sweet fragrance like an offering. The stranger closed her eyes and her face crinkled in ecstasy, as if she had never before breathed a scent so potent and lovely.

We were wary. Everything we knew of strangers suggested she was not to be trusted. But Ruth seemed harmless; a pathetic figure, not a dangerous one. Over the following days, we learned that she was a creature of habit. Every morning she came down from her room at the Alpina just before eight. We were so pleased that the Alpina had a real guest, one who had traveled to reach it, not just one of our newlywed couples staying in the honeymoon suite. In the dining room, she ate a breakfast of yogurt with stewed fruit. She took her tea with milk and four cubes of sugar, more than even our youngest children, like the only kind of pleasure she could understand was one as rudimentary as sweetness. Next, she walked in the mountains, vanishing from us for hours. She returned in early afternoon, her canvas shoes muddy, shoelaces snagged with burs. The boots she had worn the day she arrived had a small heel; in her canvas walking shoes we saw how slight she was. For the rest of the day she did what might be called poking around, strolling Hauptstrasse and popping into stores to look at this or that. She stroked the supple items in the leather goods shop, marveled at the pastries in the case at the bakery. She stood for a long time on the sidewalk outside the creamery and watched through the shop's front window as our cheesemaker poured doe's milk into basins, cut the curds and poured off the whey, pale and translucent as clouds. Her valise had been small and we quickly learned the few possessions she had brought with her. The brown boots and the canvas walking shoes, the dark crepe dress with the small white flowers, a chambray button-down and trousers, a gray shawl knit of a flimsy, fragile yarn, the straw hat with black ribbons.

She almost always had her camera with her, hanging from the strap around her neck. This interested us. We really only took portraits, whereas she photographed the smallest things. When we saw her pause to snap a picture, a warm sensation spread through us, the almost erotic pleasure of seeing her seeing us. For all her timidity, the stranger Ruth had a certain power. Her attention drew ours to those details of our town so familiar we had long ago ceased to appreciate them. With nothing but her presence she altered our familiar spaces around her.

Walking along Gartenstrasse at dusk, when the clouds were just beginning to appear, she photographed the mother-of-the-evening she'd paused to smell when she first arrived. The flower grew relentlessly, crowding everything else out. We'd grown sick of seeing it wherever we looked, but now we looked again and saw how beautiful it was, even this, our most bothersome weed, how through the clouds its pale purple petals seemed to glow. In the grove, she photographed the night-dark fruit. She even took a picture of a picture, a sepia photograph that hung in a corridor off the lobby at the Alpina: girls all in a row in front of our stone school. This picture was so old we didn't know who the girls were or whether they had been born here or had been among the people who first came to this place. They wore matching white blouses with black buttons, skirts to their ankles, braids with the silver pins fastened near the bottom instead of the nape. Their eyes were creepy the way eyes so often are in old photographs. At the end of the row, the smallest girl, much smaller than the others, scowled down at the ground. Her image was smudged, doubled: both her and a faint ghost that seemed to pull away from her. It pleased us that the stranger took notice of this photograph; she could feel our town's power even if she could not understand it. We believed our affliction began with this smudged, doubled girl, that she became a wife who became a mother who became the first of us to go.

. . .

Admittedly, it was mostly children who believed this about the girl in the photograph. This was owing to a popular legend, according to which a mother on the verge of going would not appear in photographs, or her image would be blurred or transparent. Occasionally, an anxious child or a new mother would get carried away with this superstition, a bit compulsive about it, which I would know because they would bring rolls of film to Rapid that turned out to be full of nothing but pictures of the anxious child's mother, or pictures the new mother had taken of herself in a mirror. They couldn't stop monitoring, checking to see if it was happening.

Perhaps because of my father's work, I was always especially compelled by this legend. Some of my earliest memories were of being in the darkroom, its sealed red darkness like the inside of a body. While my father worked I studied the strips of negatives that hung from clothespins on a length of twine, lilting in the airless room as if buffeted by the memories of breezes held in their images. In the negatives, people turned the opposite of themselves: black teeth, bright open mouths, eyes an obliterated white like the eyes of animals at night. The negatives terrified me, and I couldn't keep myself from looking at them. I watched my father manipulate the tools of his trade, reels and clips and tongs and rollers, working with sober grace, as if his fine-boned hands were mere extensions of his implements, his body one more mechanism in this mysterious craft. Sometimes he held me in the crook of his arm and I peered over the enamel trays, nose near to skimming the chemicals, the vinegar of stop bath so sharp it burned my eyes, and watched as he conjured faces from nothing, summoning them from their burial within the cloud-white paper. How had anyone ever come up with it? Mix this with that, soak this in the other, do all of it in the dark and call forth an image of a person as they were but are no longer. Pluck a vanished moment from the sea of the past and lock it in forever.

When our affliction came for a mother, her going was like unwinding this process: One minute she was here, as solid and real as any of us, the next her body faded, faded, until she vanished into the clouds. Gone. We all knew the stories. A mother woke her husband and told him she couldn't sleep. He turned on the bedside lamp and looked back at her and . . . nothing, no one. In the middle of the night, a mother went to fix a cup of milk for her child. A few minutes later her husband was startled by the sound of glass shattering. Outside the nursery door he found the shards, warm milk all around, his wife nowhere. A mother nursed her infant in the rocking chair, and a father lay awake listening to the rhythmic creaking of the chair until, abruptly, it ceased, and there was the child, alone in the chair.

When a mother went, we woke in the morning and sensed it. The clouds that took her touched us all, connected us all, an intimacy we had never not known. We felt her vanishing like a thread cut loose, presence turned to absence.

Ana had been beside her mother when she went. She had crept down the hallway in the night and slipped into her parents' bed. In the morning, her mother was gone. Ana's arm still bore the imprints of her fingertips; her mother had clung to her until the last possible moment. I woke up that morning to the sound of the screen door across the street slapping shut. I went to the window and there was Ana, standing on the porch, barefoot in her nightie, the silhouette of her clenched body visible through the thin material, hair unbrushed and tangled like our dolls' hair. She walked to the edge of the top step and unleashed a wail. It seemed to come from everywhere at once, down from the clouds and up from the earth and from inside me, like my bones had all along been tuned to the frequency of that wail and had now been set vibrating by it.

My own mother's going, just a week after Ana's mother's, carried no such story. Three of us went to sleep, and in the morning only two of us were there to wake. I expected our mothers' fates would draw Ana and me even closer, but I could not have been more wrong. The day after my mother's going, in the afternoon when the proceedings were finished, I tucked Walina under my arm and ran across Eschen to Ana's. I had to get away from our house, which was so empty now, my father and I settling already into the silence that was all we knew how to make together. But when I was about to cross the threshold into Ana's house, she slammed the screen door in my face. She said nothing, only stared at me through the screen with a fury that seemed to steam out of her until I retreated to my own porch to play with Walina alone, which was no good at all; I would never play with Walina again after that. I would never play with Ana again, either. She was still the first person I saw when I woke up and the last one I saw before going to sleep, but now these were only glimpses I caught: Ana stretching her arms over her head in the morning, Ana unspooling her braids at night, and always, Ana turned resolutely away from me, as if determined to expand the distance between us however she could. She didn't speak to me again until some months after our mothers went, when she had settled into her threesome with Esther and Lu, and then she spoke to me not as Ana but in their unified voice, with which they taunted and teased me for some offense I couldn't determine. I understood only that I was hated, and that this hate was as strong and intimate as the love that had preceded it. Maybe Ana hated me for the week that separated her mother's going from mine, that brief, unbridgeable interval when I still had my mother but she no longer had hers. Or maybe it was because, in the wake of our mothers' goings, when our town combed back through their lives to determine what the affliction had seen in them, why it had chosen them, it was their pairing everyone focused on. Threesomes were standard in our town, while pairings were rare, and a risk: to bind oneself so tightly to one other girl, to build your fate around hers. It suggested a certain heedlessness, and once they went we saw plainly that this heedlessness had been all over their mothering in small but significant ways. One clue about my mother everyone kept recounting was that I often turned up at school with my buckle shoes switched, right shoe on left foot, left shoe on right foot, which gave my appearance an 'unnerving' effect. My mother let me put my shoes on myself and she didn't bother to switch them if I did it wrong.

That might seem too minor to count for much, but that was just it: Our affliction was never not watching us. It saw us more clearly than we saw one another, or even ourselves, so the clues preceding a mother's going could be the smallest things, so subtle they became visible to us only in retrospect, when her going cast its clarifying light onto her past. Nothing was too insignificant to be a sign. A mother let her children cross the Graubach on the rocks when the water was a little too high, the current a little too swift. At the time it merely struck us as incautious, one of the countless small choices mothers made every day that could end in disaster but didn't. This was not a judgment. If mothers were cautious all the time, children languished; we understood this. But after she went, we found ourselves returning to that moment: the small children, the slick rocks, water rushing all around, and the mother, looking on calmly from the bank. It appeared differently to us then, no longer the sort of act that any mother might commit, but a moment that contained the singularity of her love for her children, the quality, individual to her as a fingerprint, by which our affliction had chosen her out.

Another mother refused to let anyone watch her infant for even a few minutes so she could bathe or do the shopping, not her sister or her mother or even her husband. She trusted no one but herself. She had always been tightly wound, and we had accepted this behavior as the inevitable and not altogether uncommon result of applying such a temperament to new motherhood. But after she went, we saw clearly the inimitable nature of her mothering, how her love had curdled into obsession.

One mother abandoned her impeccable garden after her child was born. She let the forest reclaim the beds of sweet pea and foxglove, allowed weeds to suffocate the rambling rose along the fence line. Another, who had never shown much diligence about anything before she became a mother, plunged herself into her basket weaving. She kept her child in his swing on the porch for hours while she wove, left the task of soothing him to the breeze instead of rocking him in her arms. One mother was seen yanking her daughter's braids for a minor offense. Another remained eerily calm when her child spit in her face.

What connected these mothers? Their clues pointed in different directions, indicating recklessness and vigilance, insufficiencies and excesses of love. Love sublimated, love coarsened, love sweetened to rot. The signs preceding a mother's going were individual to her. They did not add up to something so crude as criteria, as a lesson or a rule. But once a mother went, we saw it, something out of balance in the nature of her love for her children that set her apart. Had she fallen out of balance on her own, and had her fall drawn the affliction to her? Or was she born afflicted, and all along, through her girlhood and her adolescence, her marriage and her pregnancies and, as long as it lasted, her motherhood, had she carried it inside her, and had it worked upon her until there was nothing in her that was not touched by it? We couldn't say. We knew only that she was no longer meant to be here, that we were not meant to have her, keep her, and her going was the proof of this. Her absence left a cavity, a wound, as if our affliction had opened us to perform a necessary extraction. But like any wound, it healed. For a time, we could still see the traces of it, still feel the tenderness in the places where she used to be. But soon enough a day came when we probed for the spot, and we discovered that we could no longer find it, or even remember how it had felt.

Every year on my birthday, my father took Di, Marie, and me to afternoon tea at the Alpina. We'd been doing this since I was a little girl, when it was what every girl did on her birthday. We were still doing it the year the stranger arrived in town; my sixteenth birthday had been the month before. My father hadn't put together that I'd outgrown it and I couldn't bring myself to tell him. Just as when we were girls, Di, reeking of her older sister's bergamot perfume, snatched up the best pastries before the rest of us could get to them, while Marie put on a prim display, dabbing at invisible crumbs on her lips. I let my tea steep until it was nearly black. The last supply had been several months earlier and the Alpina had run out of the tea sachets Mr. Phillips brought, which came wrapped in pale blue paper with an illustration of tea leaves embossed in gold. For now, we drank a local brew, raspberry leaves and nettle, the loose leaves writhing at the bottom of the hot water like things long-dead, revived. Halfway through tea, as I always did, I excused myself to use the restroom, but I didn't go to the restroom. I went down the opposite corridor to look at the photograph of the girls. I stared at it, at them, and thought that they were long dead now, all of them except the little one on the end, the blurred runt, who had, perhaps, done something other than die. And I wondered what our affliction had recognized in her, or cultivated in her until it was all of her.

We circled the stranger. Suddenly, lots of us began taking morning walks into the mountains, and the usually deserted paths became positively crowded. One day in the caf, Marie told Di and me that the previous afternoon, 'seeing as it was such a fine day,' she had decided to take her cello to Feldpark to practice the piece we uppers would be performing at the next recital, and the stranger 'happened to be there taking her photographs' and had complimented her playing. Di had taken to wearing a straw hat from her sister's bureau around town, an obvious ploy to get the stranger to remark upon their similar taste. I spotted Ana, Esther, and Lu sitting on the bench below the stranger's window at the Alpina, gossiping and laughing loudly at regular intervals to show what a fun time they were having. Mothers could often be seen pushing prams down the sidewalks of Hauptstrasse, our principal commercial street, during the afternoon hours when Ruth poked around. Ruth smiled at the babies and sometimes said something like 'Precious' or 'How adorable' to the mothers, and the mothers thanked her politely, though the vague, aloof quality of Ruth's smile and these rather vapid things she said only confirmed how limited she was, this woman who was old enough to be a mother but was instead here all alone. Husbands lingered just outside the stranger's vision in late afternoon, and when the clouds began to gather they approached her as if they just so happened to be passing by and offered to escort her back to the Alpina. They were the most discreet in their circling. They didn't want their wives to suspect the way the stranger was working upon them. They hardly understood it themselves. At night during lovemaking, when wives removed the silver pins from their braids and pierced their husbands' skin, the husbands had begun to imagine it was the stranger doing this to them.

I circled her like the rest of us. I was always trying to encounter her, and our town was small enough that often I succeeded. I followed her into the grocery and studied the contents of her basket. Crackers, a sewing kit, a jar of olives. I hated olives, but after seeing them in her basket, I purchased a jar. That night I locked my bedroom door and ate them one at a time; I chewed slowly and methodically, sucked the oil from the fruits, brine like salt water for rinsing a sore throat, and spat the pits into my palm, trying to make them taste to me the way they must to her, like my mouth was strange to me, like it was hers.

I slipped out during my shift and went to Feldpark and sure enough there she was, on one of the benches that surrounded the fountain with the statue of the crying woman at its center. I sat on the bench next to hers and pulled out of my book bag the sheet music for the piece for the next recital. I pretended to study it intently, though really my focus was all on Ruth. I wanted so badly to engage her, but I didn't want to seem intrusive or desperate, and to my delight it was she who spoke to me.

'What's that?' she asked.

I told her the title of the piece. 'It's the name of a river elsewhere,' I explained. It said so in a brief introductory note at the top of the music. The piece was meant to evoke the journey of this river, which started as a small mountain spring and flowed past the village where the composer had lived, or perhaps lived still, before emptying into the sea.

'Is that so?' She looked amused. It occurred to me that this river might be well-known elsewhere, in which case my attempt to appear knowledgeable had actually achieved the opposite.

'Yes,' I said. 'Someplace far from here. A place with seasons.' I couldn't help it, I wanted her to know we knew things about the rest of the world. We may have lacked some of the things they had, their films and magazines and periodicals; our library contained just what was useful, picture books and learn-to-reads for small children, arithmetic and medical and botany texts, but that was our choice. Mr. Phillips would bring us anything we asked for. If we wanted a novel, or a book of history, or a popular film and a projector to watch it on, all we would have had to do was ask and at the next supply he would have it, but we didn't. What could the stories and histories of people elsewhere offer us? Only their music, wordless, was of any use to us.

'I came here from a place like that,' she said.

I got shy then. Mr. Phillips never spoke to us about elsewhere, and while I supposed there was no rule against it, and pleased as I was that she had confided this in me, I couldn't help but feel she was telling me things she shouldn't, and I didn't know how to respond.

'You'd love to see the seasons,' she continued.

Luckily, the clouds had started to come out by then, creeping among the trees and spreading over the fields. I looked at them pointedly. 'We should probably be going.' I gathered my things and hurried away.

Our conversation that afternoon reminded me of something I hadn't thought about in the longest time. I said earlier that it never snowed in our town, but that wasn't entirely true. There was a time, not long after my mother went, when a cold and unfamiliar air slipped over the mountains. For days it lingered, each day colder than the last. We huddled under blankets, gripped cups of steaming tea to keep warm. On the fourth day we awoke to find our town dusted in white. We stepped out of our houses into the streets and stared in silence. We knew it was snow, though I don't remember us saying the word. Before my father could tell me not to, I scooped some into my hands. Pure lightness, pure cold. I wanted to taste it, but I didn't dare, and anyway by then my father had noticed what I was doing and I opened my palms and let the snow fall. We breathed in deeply, trying to pin down the snow's peculiar and powerful scent. It took us time to realize it had no scent at all, but covered over and erased all of our town's familiar scents: We smelled not presence but absence. We fetched shovels and baskets and wheelbarrows; children brought their toy pails. We swept the snow into these vessels and carried them to the Graubach. We climbed down the embankment and tossed the snow in the river and watched it melt to nothing as the water carried it off.

Another time, a strange bird appeared in town, a large white specimen with gray wings and translucent yellow eyes. Someone said they thought it came from the coast. A seagull. It hopped from rooftop to rooftop, its call piercing and relentless. Children snatched up stones and grabbed their slingshots, and in no time one of them hit the mark. The bird dropped to the ground, but it was still alive. A father scooped it up and cradled it in his arms, big as a baby. Its battered breast heaved; the feathers there were stained pink, and the father had blood on his fingers, oily and bright. We followed him to the Graubach. He took the bird in both hands and knelt at the river's edge. He plunged it under the cold clear water and held it there until it went limp in his hands. Then he released it and it floated downstream.

Sometimes I didn't go looking for Ruth. I stayed at Rapid for my shift, though often I ended up seeing her anyway, because she came in to purchase film. Di and Marie were so jealous that I got this additional access to her, which meant she grew especially comfortable with me. To my great pleasure, I had witnessed Ana try to strike up a conversation with her at the bakery, going on with unusual enthusiasm about the tea cake, and offering Ruth a piece of hers, which Ruth popped into her mouth without carrying the exchange any further. Whereas with me she had grown almost chatty. While I rang up her film, she asked me questions: Were we getting used to her? Did she still seem as strange to us as when she first arrived? Our town was a small and gossipy place, and she trusted me not to go blabbing about what she'd asked and the reassurances she'd sought.

If he heard us, my father would come out from the darkroom in his black apron to join us, which was unusual for him. He never came out to talk with customers. He was content, or maybe resigned, to spend his days developing images of everyone else's lives, washing the prints with a gentle touch that had made me long as a child for him to hold me with as much tenderness, and to wonder why he wouldn't, or couldn't. But even he couldn't resist the novelty of a stranger. Ruth seemed to sense his fundamental reticence and she made herself mild to match his mildness. She was just a hobbyist when it came to photography, not an expert like him, and she was always full of questions for him. She asked him how to take advantage of the diffuse light in our town, which was so different from the stark glare and shadow to which she was accustomed, how to utilize various angles and perspectives and to capture motion and reflections. As the days passed, my father answered her with increasing comfort and detail. He told her about the rule of thirds, the virtues of patterns and symmetry, and how to use leading lines, fences or paths or shadows, to draw the viewer deep into the image.

There were limits to her trust, though. She bought so much film from us. She must have been accumulating quite the pile of finished rolls in her room at the Alpina, but she never brought them in.

'We develop, too,' I told her one afternoon, in case she wasn't aware. I was desperate to see her photographs, to see us as we appeared to her.

'Great,' she said, but I could see she had no intention of bringing them. I wanted to tell her it wasn't like where she came from, that we were trustworthy and discreet, that whatever was in her film, I wouldn't tell anyone, but I didn't know quite how to frame it.

'That's pretty,' she said. She pointed at the bangle on my wrist, gold inlaid with small red stones. Like the other girls, I had been taking extra care with my appearance since her arrival. I'd purchased the bangle at the Op Shop with my allowance when I was a girl. I hardly ever wore it, it was clunky and got in the way, but I'd put it on for her, and here she was, admiring it.

'Thanks,' I said coolly, as if her compliment hardly mattered to me.

'I used to have a bracelet just like that.'

I doubted whatever bauble she'd had elsewhere had been 'just like' mine, but I smiled warmly at her. 'Here.' I wriggled the bangle off my wrist and held it out to her.

She looked stricken. 'I couldn't.'

'Please. I want you to have it.'

She hesitated, then relented. She held out her hand and I slid the bangle onto her wrist.

I was far from the only one to give her gifts. Children approached her shyly but proudly with flower crowns and twine lanyards and colored wax drawings. Much to Marie's consternation, her little brother presented Ruth with a toad in a jar, still slick with mud from the riverbank. We uppers plied her no less eagerly than the younger children. Tess offered her a watercolor of the Graubach, trees and clouds reflected on its surface, silver fish slipping through the waters beneath. Esther gave her a kerchief embroidered with a stem of the mother-of-the-evening that so captivated her. From Henry she received a bottle of our local liquor infused with rose hips from his mother's garden. From Peter, carvings of forest animals, a goat, a bee-eater, a coiled viper, sanded smooth as milk. Every morning when she walked past the bakery, the proprietress rushed out with a different pastry, a raspberry bun one day, a slice of lemon cake the next. When Ruth sent her clothes for washing at the Alpina, the laundress darned the threadbare heels of her socks. Even my father gave her a small token, a photography handbook that had sat forever on the shelf in our parlor. She flipped slowly through its yellowed pages, brushed her fingertips along its dog-ears and underlines and notes in silver pencil. 'But you love this,' she said. 'I can see you do. Look how you've marked it.' She tried to hand it back to him, but he shook his head. She was unaccustomed to such generosity and we could see it made her uneasy. She tried to refuse many of our gifts, but we wouldn't hear of it. We wanted her to have beautiful things. It pleased us to watch her see, taste, touch all we had to offer. We hammered the head from a barrel of our white cheese, drained the brine, and gave her the first slice from the round. It carried the flavors of this place: milk from goats who fed on the forest's ferns and saplings and mushrooms, barrels made from the wood of trees that grew high on the mountains, and which held the clouds fast in their grain. We gathered around and watched her consume it.

She was learning. She had begun to open the window of her room at the Alpina at night to let in the clouds. We thought of them filling her room, settling over her as she slept, her hair let loose from the braid she had begun to wear, of her breathing them in and out. One day when she came into Rapid for film, she didn't stack her coins on the counter, she dropped them into my palm, making sure to let our fingertips touch. Hers were smooth yet rough, like the flat stones we skipped into the Graubach as children, and I tried to maintain my composure, not to let her see how her touch thrilled me.

'How old are you?' she asked that day.

'Sixteen. I'm an upper. I'll be done with school next month.'

'And then?'

I was a bit thrown by the question. 'Then everything. My whole life.'

'You're looking forward to it?'

'Of course.' I smiled. I didn't want her to see how sad I found it that this was a question she thought it necessary to ask, that elsewhere it was apparently not a given that a girl would await the unfolding of her life with great anticipation. 'We uppers have all been saying how lucky we are to be this age for your visit. It's such an important time for us. You being here makes it that much more special.'

'How nice.' She smiled, but her smile was strained, and I could tell she didn't really grasp what I was telling her.

It wasn't exactly true that 'we uppers' had all been saying this. It was really just something I had thought to myself, that having the stranger here at this critical time heightened it. Soon we would be done with school. In a few short years, most of us would be husbands and wives, and then fathers and mothers. In the caf, Di, Marie, and I talked incessantly about our hopes. Which boys did we want to marry? How old did we think we would be when we became mothers? How many children did we want to have? Di's older sister had taught us to kiss by practicing on each other, an exercise she insisted provided the necessary preparation, though I was skeptical that this thing I did with Di and Marie on a rug strewn with cookie crumbs from our midnight snacking, tangling our tongues passionlessly together, had anything to do with kissing a boy who might make me a mother.

Though I participated convincingly in the conversations with Di and Marie, and in Di's sister's 'lessons,' in truth I was terrified that my silver hairpin would never leave my braid to pierce a man's skin, that I was destined to be a childless spinster. It was Ana who had planted this fear in me. She had done it without a word, years earlier. We were in eighth and had been assigned desks next to each other. Ana had recently been the first of us to start wearing her hair in a single braid down her back, with a few tendrils left out at the front to frame her face. She ignored me absolutely, and I tried to do the same to her, but I couldn't help myself from stealing glances at her braid, so fat and solid my hands tingled at the sight of it, filled with an urge to wrap around it and squeeze. One day, she angled her notebook a bit more to the side of her desk than usual, and I couldn't help but steal a glance at that, too. Mixed in with the spirals and flowers drawn in the margins, I saw a list of names. *Nadia. Daphne. Teresa.* When she caught me looking, she rolled her eyes and moved her arm to cover the page. I thought at first these were names she would have preferred for herself, *Ana* being so plain, but a few days later I spotted another list. *Raphael. Gregory. Daniel.* I put it together then that these were names for children. All at once it dawned on me that other girls did something I didn't. Their minds wandered naturally to their futures. Di had a pad filled with sketches for her wedding dress. Marie often looked around censoriously at our peers and declared that when she was a mother, she would never let her children do this or wear that; Marie had been born to be a mother, I thought with irritation, and with envy. But I had never imagined my wedding, or what rules I would impose upon my children, or what their names might be. And Ana had known this about me, sensed it in me. She acted like I'd pried by looking at her notebook, but she'd positioned it where I could see it; she'd wanted me to look, to know she knew this about me. How had she known it? Was it because she had tasted my blood, because I was in her and she was in me? That night in bed, I set about trying to imagine the phases that lay ahead of me, but I came up empty. I considered each of the boys in our year and the years above and below. Could I marry any of them? No, I couldn't, impossible, not even the ones I liked, who I would be too shy to marry. All I could imagine, because it required no imagination at all, was a future in which I continued to live in my father's house and work in his store, day after year until I was old. What reason could there be for this except that my fate did not contain what the others' fates did, that their future husbands and children called to them, while I had none to call to me?

This was a devastating thing to fear. When a woman became a mother, she revealed herself. A meek girl became a mother who screamed at her children when they disobeyed her. She hadn't thought herself capable of such rage. Now she was incapable of ridding herself of it. A girl who had always been cold and aloof coddled her children. She covered the inches of them in kisses and craved nothing so much as the feeling of their tears soaking her as she soothed them. A girl became a mother who stayed or a mother who went, an outcome that surprised us, or didn't. Impossible to predict, what motherhood would bring out of a woman, what it would show her about herself, the end to which it would carry her.

Every few years we had a girl who did not marry, or mother, exempting herself from the risks the rest of us bore, and we pitied her. She was safe, but she was also deprived. These solitary women kept to themselves. They lived alone in houses on our town's peripheries, wove the baskets necessary to support themselves and otherwise devoted themselves to obscure interests. Mr. Phillips brought them the oddest special orders. For one, packets of seeds that she sprinkled indiscriminately in her yard and garden, and which sprouted creepers that grew in dense mats and bound themselves to every surface. She did nothing to curtail this growth; she allowed the plants to cover her lawn and climb the walls of her house until it was completely concealed. The creepers sent runners underground, and they spread in this manner into town, tendrils climbing walls and suckering to cobbles in our streets. We were constantly ripping them down, trying to beat them back, lest they overtake everything. A mystery to us why she found it a worthwhile plant to cultivate. For another, Mr. Phillips brought a dried herb with a musty odor, which she wrapped in white paper and smoked. She flung the spent remains of her habit here, there, and everywhere, often with the ember still burning. A careless woman, no children to make her cautious.

Then there were those few women who did marry, but to whom no children came. Our hygienist, a twitchy, nervous slip of a woman who chewed her lower lip voraciously; we assumed the problem lay with her, that no child could settle in such an anxious womb. And of course there was Sally, whose husband, a notorious drunkard, had died in a foolish accident years before I was born, when Sally was quite young. Sally's behavior, her desperation to be needed, her girlish clothes, all of it was symptomatic of her childless state and how it had stunted her. She never knew the truth of herself, not really, because she had never offered herself to our affliction, never had a child to teach her who she was.

Ruth had been with us for some weeks now, and we started to get excited. Did she plan to stay on more permanently? Could she? We supposed there was no rule against it. We had tried, at first, to manage our expectations and moderate our feelings, but now we permitted our minds to drift pleasurably to thoughts of having her with us always, on supply days and at our weddings and even signing up for the meal train when a baby was born. We wanted her to love us. We wanted her to be our stranger forever.

We started to get the feeling a mother would be going soon. It had been months since the last one. Our affliction was unpredictable. It followed no set pattern or cycle. Sometimes it seemed to settle into a rhythm, a mother going just before each supply, say, but then three would go in a rush, or half a year would pass without any going at all. Still, in a typical year we lost three or four mothers, and while we could never determine exactly when it would come, we sensed its approach. We grew unsettled. The clouds seemed to carry an imminence, a brewing pressure, as if they were growing restless and our agitation was a mere reflection of that restlessness.

My practicing had fallen off since Ruth arrived, and I needed to pick it back up if I wanted to be ready for the recital. One day I took my violin to the Graubach. I climbed over the embankment, kicked off my sandals, hitched my skirt and walked in, ankle deep. The water was cold and swift and so clear it magnified the rocks on the riverbed, which were coated in moss that swayed in the current. The forest pressed in from both sides like the river were a secret it was devoted to keeping. I had come to the Graubach hoping for inspiration, since the piece we were learning was about the course of a river. As I began to play, I tried to let the music enter me. I thought of Ana, who hardly practiced but was still the most gifted player in our year, 'a natural' as we all said; I conjured her furious bowing, like her instrument was a beast she was trying to tame, or a lover she wanted to make submit, and how the music seemed to bring her deepest self, the one I remembered from our girlhoods, fleetingly to her surface, where it flickered like light on water, so quick I could never quite catch it. But even with my feet in the river, I couldn't really figure out how to do this. My playing was so workmanlike. When I tried to push it, I only made mistakes. I hadn't been playing long when Ruth appeared on the bank.

'Please don't stop on my account,' she said when she reached me. But I felt weird performing for her, and I kept my violin dangling at my side, just above the water. 'Please,' she said again. 'I've never heard that piece before. I'd love to.' She slipped the canvas walking shoes off her feet and tossed them up the embankment, rolled the cuffs of her trousers and joined me with her feet in the water. Barefoot I could see how small her feet were. It was a lie, what she'd said. She had heard the piece before; Marie had played it for her just a few days ago in Feldpark. She looked at me so hopefully, even hungrily, and I understood that she had been trying to convince me to play for her any way she could. She was that desperate for the beauty we had to offer, and she thought she had to lie to get it. I lifted my violin to my chin and began the piece again from the beginning. She closed her eyes and listened, arms wrapped tightly around herself. The composition was mournful, an airy prelude that gave way to a melody in a minor key. At times it shifted into a major scale, and you thought maybe it would stay there, but after a few bars it shifted back. When I came to the end, she jerked her head, as if roused from a dream.

'You play so beautifully,' she said. There were tears in her eyes. I didn't have the heart to tell her how mediocre I was by our standards. I couldn't imagine what the playing must be like elsewhere for her to find mine beautiful.

She stepped out a little farther into the water and dug her toes into the velvety silt. She turned her gaze away from me and cast it downstream. The cuffs of her trousers were getting wet, but she seemed not to notice. 'Do you ever wonder where it goes?'

'I know where it goes.' I had spoken a bit curtly and felt badly about it, but I was taken aback, and a little insulted, that she would think we wouldn't know something like that.

'Oh?'

'It goes down the mountain. It goes elsewhere.'

One afternoon when I was practicing my violin behind the counter at Rapid, Ana, Esther, and Lu walked in holding hands like a paper chain.

'Wow, you're really coming along, Vera,' Ana said.

'*Brava,*' Esther said.

'Only moderately painful,' Lu said.

Their threesome had started the hand-holding trend earlier in the year and now all the upper girls were doing it. Liese, Rachel, and Cecily. Julia, June, and Lila. The idea was to step all in unison, and to sway your hips in unison, too. This trend spoke to the competing impulses of that period for us, to plunge into our adult lives, to leave girlhood behind, but also to cling to it. Even Di, Marie, and I had started going hand in hand down the school corridors and around town, one of my hands in Di's sweaty hand, the other in Marie's firm grip. I felt self-conscious when we did it because we'd adopted the trend so late, and because I couldn't tell if we looked as awkward as I felt, if it showed that we lacked the intimacy a threesome ought to possess. When Ana, Esther, and Lu did it, it looked flawless. They moved like a single, three-bodied girl, though I couldn't help but wonder if Ana, too, found her threesome lacking compared to what we'd shared and was just better at hiding it.

'Do you detect an odor in here, Vera?' Ana asked.

Esther and Lu snickered. This was a reference to an episode that had transpired when we were in second, of which it seemed Ana would never tire of reminding me. One night, sweeping the floor at home, I had found a hair in the dustpan too long and dark to be my own. I wove it into one of my braids and for days I kept the braids in; I didn't undo them to sleep, or to bathe, terrified of losing that hair, which maybe, maybe, had been my mother's. After a few days, my hair grew shiny and stiff enough with grease that I didn't even need the ribbons at the ends of the braids to keep them from unraveling. I loved the feeling of it, that dark strand like a secret I carried, like I protected it and it protected me. But one day at school, Ana marched up to me in front of all of us in the caf and declared, 'Your head stinks.' As soon as she said it, I understood what a terrific and humiliating error I had made. Was this the sort of strange thing my mother would have done? Had I done it because I was like her? Or had I done it because I had no mother to tell me not to, no mother to notice and correct the oddities all children possess? Was I the way I was because I had a mother, or because I didn't? Everyone in the caf stared at Ana and me, and we stared at each other. Only the two of us knew that a silent conversation was passing between us, in which I said, *I could tell them right now. I could shout it. Ana eats dirt!* And Ana said, *We both know you wouldn't dare.*

Now, standing across from Ana in Rapid, I wanted to deliver some sharp retort. To say, *What an original comment, Ana,* or, *I hadn't detected any odor before you came in,* but once again I didn't dare, and I only shook my head.

Ana separated from Esther and Lu and approached the counter. She loomed over me. Her bigness and my smallness had seemed like destiny when we were a pairing, opposites bound together, but now it only made her more intimidating.

'Dropping off and picking up,' she said. She reached into her book bag and passed three rolls into my hands, the brushing of our fingertips causing my breath to catch like always. I fetched the envelope with her pictures from the Out basket and handed it to her. Ana, Esther, and Lu didn't leave the store after that, though. They stayed right on the other side of the counter, huddled together, and started going through the pictures, giggling and reminiscing about the revelry captured in them and complimenting one another on how nice they looked, doing that thing where you make your conversation louder and more pointed when you're excluding someone. Suddenly Ana paused and turned to me. 'You didn't look at these, did you?' she asked accusingly.

'Of course not.' Never mind that it wasn't possible to check the photographs for misprints and pile them tidily into the envelope without looking at them, which obviously Ana knew. I was pretty sure half the reason she took so many photos was so I'd have to see them: Ana lying in the fields with Esther and Lu when the sun broke through, and applying lavender masks to their faces in Ana's bedroom, and splashing in the shallows of the Graubach with three boys from the year above ours. Seeing that image had sent a shiver through me, like waking from a deep sleep. Had Ana pricked a boy yet, and replaced the taste of my blood with his?

'She totally did,' Esther said.

'Do you think she takes them home at night?' Lu said.

The shop door opened and they glanced back. It was Ruth. Ana sighed and placed her tented hands on the counter. 'These will be ready when?' She gestured with her chin at the rolls of film in the In basket.

'End of the week.' I felt Ana's eyes on me, but couldn't raise mine to meet hers.

'How rapid.'

Ana, Esther, and Lu said an overly sweet hello to Ruth, then joined hands and floated out of the store.

Ruth had come for another role of film. 'What was that about?' she asked as I rang her up.

'Just Ana being Ana.'

'You two aren't friends?'

I laughed at that. 'Our mothers were, and we used to be. I guess that's why she gives me such a hard time, just to be clear we're not anymore.'

'You said it's just you and your father. Your mother . . .'

'She's gone.'

'Gone,' she repeated.

I could tell she wanted me to go on, to explain, but I couldn't begin to think what to say to her. Instead I just nodded.

She closed her eyes for several beats, then opened them. 'I'm so sorry, Vera.' She looked at me with the saddest expression.

I did my best to smile appreciatively at this sentiment, which was clearly well-intentioned. 'You're all set,' I said, passing the film into her hands.

Dinner at our house that night was canned beef soup warmed briefly on the stove and still tanging of metal. At the table, my father and I asked each other about our days and confirmed that they had been fine, and after that we ate without speaking. In a few minutes we had finished, and we rinsed and dried and stacked our bowls, careful not to let them clank together. We were so quiet all the time. We moved as if there were a baby asleep somewhere in the house we were trying not to wake. After dinner, we drifted to our separate spaces. My father read and dozed on the sofa in the parlor. He always sat in the same spot; the upholstery, green with pink flowers, had worn away there. I retreated to my bedroom. A few hours later, I heard the stairs creaking under his soundless footfalls, and he appeared in the hallway outside my room. He didn't come in, just stood in the doorway, one hand patting the jamb in a slow rhythm. He was tall enough that what fine hairs remained on his head nearly skimmed the lintel, and he carried his height and his long limbs uncomfortably, as if he had awoken just today to find himself in this body, and was still growing accustomed to it. His features, too, were overlarge and protruding, so that his face seemed to be perpetually grappling with what to do with it all. I looked nothing like him. My own features were small and sharp, 'so mousy,' as I had once heard Ana fake-whisper to Esther and Lu in the caf. I assumed I must take after my mother, and sometimes I studied my face in the mirror and tried to find her face in mine, but I didn't know what to look for. 'Well, good night,' he said. He patted the jamb a final time before turning and walking down the hall.

I couldn't stop thinking that night about what Ruth had said in

Rapid, about how sorry she was for me, and how sad she looked when she said it. I hated that she felt badly for me, that she couldn't see it was I who ought to feel sorry for her, though I knew this wasn't her fault, that her life had afforded her no opportunity to see things any other way. I told her I had no mother, and she couldn't see beyond my personal deprivations. All she could think was that I'd had no mother to soothe my fevers and mend my scrapes, no mother to go to when I bled for the first time. She couldn't comprehend that a mother's going belonged to all of us, or that loss was the smallest part of it, because in losing her, we received everything else. Our affliction opened us to pain, yes, but also to heights of beauty, and of love, that people elsewhere would never know because they did not know what it was to love in the shadow of our affliction, our love deepened and made wild by the threat that hovered over it. Our affliction was terrible, but it was not as terrible as living without it.

Which was not to say I didn't feel the absence of a mother in my life. When I thought *mother,* a feeling came over me like lying under quilts at night in a cold room. Sometimes I looked at a certain object in our house, a plate with a pink rose painted at the center and a chip on the gold rim, or at something in town, the middle swing at Feldpark or a woman's brown shawl, and the object seemed weighted, full of something I couldn't name, heavy like Walina when I left her out and she soaked up the clouds. Sometimes when my stomach churned and twisted, a peculiar notion came over me that my mother had gone to live inside me. She floated in the dark sea there, a creature I held safe but could not access.

I was always on the lookout for mothers and daughters alone together, private moments that hinted at what it was like between them. Mothers and daughters brought something out of each other. I had seen girls unleash themselves with their mothers, like their mothers were a potion that stripped them of their ability to behave. I think of the time I saw Rachel, the most timid girl in our year, shriek and shake her fists at her mother on their front porch until she panted. Or the time we were about to go onstage at a recital and a bird on a branch released a sticky white glob that landed in Di's braid. When her mother ran up from the grass with a wet handkerchief to wipe it away, Di rolled her eyes and sassed, 'I've *got it*'; she combed the mess out of her hair with her own fingers rather than give her mother the satisfaction of being needed. Or the mother and daughter I watched once in the bakery, seated across from each other at one of the small round tables, a slice of raspberry curd tart in front of each of them. I heard the mother snap, 'I can't believe you,' and the daughter whisper with cold heat, 'I hate you.' Yet all the while, beneath the table, their skirts were hitched up over knees crossed at identical angles and their ankles bounced together in time. After they spoke their angry words, mother and daughter each pressed their index fingers down over loose crumbs on their plates and brought their fingers to their lips to eat them. A mother was a chance to hate someone as much as you loved them, caring and wounding, a push and pull that only tightened the knot that bound you. While I envied the other girls their mothers, it felt right to me that I didn't have mine. Difficult, but comforting, the way I supposed one's own life always feels. Besides, it made no sense to contemplate some other life in which I got to keep my mother, because in such a life, our town would not have been what it was.

But it was unreasonable to expect Ruth to understand any of this. Even Mr. Phillips, who had been visiting us my whole life, had slips that reminded us how little he grasped about us. I'm thinking of this habit he had, part of his routine when he arrived each supply. I see us descending to meet him on those mornings. Mothers wore their babies wrapped to their chests with lengths of cotton cloth. Fathers pushed wheelbarrows loaded high with baskets for Mr. Phillips to sell. Old women carried gifts for him, a handkerchief with a cross-stitch monogram, a cheese and cress sandwich for his journey home. Children skipped excitedly along the edges of the supply road. Little girls rubbed at their scalps, braids done so tightly on these mornings they throbbed. Little boys thwacked at low-hanging branches with sticks, sending water raining down. Older boys donned their work clothes, ready to show off how much they could carry back up to town, while we older girls dressed prettily and impractically in whatever was in style at the moment, long, flowing skirts that caught on our flimsy sandals, blouses that laced up the back and left us trying to conceal our panting on the steep terrain; we dressed for Mr. Phillips, eager to present to him our newest selves, how much we'd grown and changed since his last visit.

When the train slowed to a stop, one of the car doors slid open and Mr. Phillips appeared in his linen suit, with his trim mustache, the shiny red tops of his ears, the bald spot on his head pink and white like rose quartz. He stepped down gingerly onto the gravel beside the tracks and began to get everything arranged, unfolding the table and chair and settling the legs into the gravel in front of the dark, gaping mouth of the freight car. As he went about this task, he glanced up every few seconds to survey us. These glances were brief and easy to dismiss as Mr. Phillips being happy to see us, or as a betrayal of self-consciousness, one of him in front of all of us. But I once caught him doing one of these glances and then, as if troubled by something he'd seen, immediately looking back up to confirm it. Not long after that he was ready, and he sat behind the table and we came up one family

at a time to deliver our baskets and pick up our orders and place requests. It was some time into this process when a father and his children approached the table and Mr. Phillips asked the youngest child,
'Where's your mama this morning?' The odd thing was, he asked
this as if he'd only just noticed the woman's absence, whereas I could
have sworn he'd registered it the moment, nearly an hour earlier,
when he did that double take. When the child told Mr. Phillips that
her mother had gone, I was near enough to see his expression shift.
He closed his eyes just like Ruth had in Rapid, as if you could shut out
a truth and will it undone. His mouth tightened, and he gulped like
swallowing dry bread. This response of his was just like when someone died. After all, people died here the same as anywhere, and when
they did we told Mr. Phillips, and often we cried with him. We felt a
comfort with him that was hard to explain; we felt better, lighter, after
we shared our sorrows with him, like he loaded them onto the train
and carried them away.

In this instance, he knew the mother had not died, but he could
not grasp what had happened to her instead, nor find any way to feel
about it except this simple sadness and a wishing against it, no different than if the mother had caught a fever or fallen from a great height.
He couldn't access what it meant to us, and if he couldn't, it was unreasonable to expect Ruth, who had known us only weeks, to grasp it
even half as well.

It was five days later that I awoke with the unsettled sense that something had altered in the night while we slept. I went to my window.
Down below I saw Eschen as it always was at that early hour, the cobblestones wet and shining, scraps of clouds hovering over the street
and rooftops. Nobody out, everything quiet, except for Ana, pacing

the sidewalk. When I saw her out there, I knew for sure a mother had gone. Ever since her own mother went, Ana was always the first one out on Eschen on these mornings. She strode back and forth on the sidewalk with her hands crossed tightly against her chest. It was a short street with only a few houses, and each time she reached the end of it she turned slowly, as if out of some tedious obligation, and continued walking in the other direction. As I watched her, just at the level on my own chest where Ana's arms crossed over hers, some smaller, reflected movement seemed to occur inside me, energy shuttling back and forth like thread on a spindle. Though she was out for anyone to see, I knew I was not supposed to watch her, though I also couldn't shake the feeling, or maybe just the hope, that Ana performed this ritual for me to see. After some time she paused her pacing. She squatted down and reached her hand in among the ferns that grew along the sidewalk. She scooped up a fistful of wet dirt and closed her hand around it, then stood and continued her walking. Without breaking stride, she brought the dirt to her mouth. She looked up at my window then and caught me staring. She gazed at me with a faint smile. Then she bent down, picked up a stone, and hurled it. A loud crack ricocheted through the morning's silence. I flinched, and when I looked back, a delicate fissure had appeared in my windowpane, so fine you would never notice it if you didn't know it was there. Ana stood below, admiring her handiwork. I could make out flecks of dirt on her lips, and I knew that inside her mouth the seams between her teeth were black. I wondered if she would ever stop punishing me for knowing who she was beneath the girl she had made herself into after her mother went, and if I would want her to.

My father and I washed and dressed and went out into the street. Mild weather had blown in during the night, and Eschen stood windless and almost warm, quiet but for the plinking of water from trees into the grass. Nearly everyone was out by then, and we began to walk, our numbers growing as we turned onto larger streets and were joined by others. Who had gone? Was it our sister, our teacher, one of our threesome? Our own grown daughter? We were desperate to know, but also desperate not to know, to remain innocent just a little while longer of the news, the name. This morning our walk took us across town, down Hauptstrasse and Gartenstrasse and finally to Bergstrasse, one of our loveliest streets, boxes of cranesbill and creeping Jenny in the windows, the sidewalks lined with white hibiscus, and here we joined the growing assembly on a freshly trimmed front lawn. The father and his children came out promptly, a little boy and a sixth-year girl I recognized by her sharp widow's peak. Father, son, and daughter took in the crowd with identical stunned expressions, like animals after a shot and before they fell. The girl sat on the top porch step, arms wrapped tightly around her knees, a red shawl her mother must have knitted over her trembling shoulders. The father lifted the boy onto the porch rail and held him steady around the waist. The boy wore a ribbed undershirt, underpants, and yellow galoshes. He kicked his heels against the balusters, causing the boots to drop off his feet into the grass. The father saw this but didn't move, so the daughter fetched the boots and slid them back onto her brother's feet. The boy seemed hardly to notice this intervention.

As we stood on the lawn, waiting for the proceedings to get underway, the mothers swayed and chattered in their threes and in larger groups. At first, the consensus was that this mother was a surprise. But after some discussion, we agreed we'd noticed a certain shift in her of late. We always found the indications in the end; it was just a matter of combing through the past carefully enough. In this case, one recent incident stood out. A week earlier, the boy who now sat on the porch rail in his underclothes had opened his lunch pail in the caf at school and lifted from it a brown apple core. The pail also contained two crusts of bread and a half-eaten square of cheese, hardened and yellowed and bearing the imprints of his baby teeth. These were the remains of his lunch from the day before. His mother had forgotten to empty out and repack the pail. The boy's teacher had given him her own lunch to eat, chicken salad, bright yellow and studded with sultanas, which he picked at nervously, the teacher's food. It was a mistake any mother could make. What mother hadn't, at some point, lost track of time and left her child waiting on the school's stone steps long after the last bell, or sent them off with a thermos of juice instead of soup? So many details, so much remembering, their minds ticking away with it all. Mothers were tired and, a word I heard again and again that morning, *harried*, which made me think of hair, as if motherhood were a coarse coat women grew. Only now did we suspect that the lunch pail incident hadn't been an ordinary moment of distraction, that the mother had begun to perceive our affliction circling her, and all of her attention had been absorbed by it. Mothers often sensed their goings before they came, though how often was difficult to determine, because it wasn't talked about, at least not openly, though mothers whispered of strange premonitions, unsettling changes: a body that could no longer be ruled by her mind, a mind obsessed with her body's dissolution.

We got on with it. The mothers went into the house and gathered the woman's possessions: her clothing and jewelry and shoes, the articles of her hobbies. They piled these into wheelbarrows, and we tried to steal glances at the piles without appearing too eager before our young men carted the barrows away. Once the house was emptied of the woman's personal effects, the fathers went in. While the mothers had worked haphazardly, snatching things up as they encountered them, the fathers were scrupulous. They went room by room, opened every closet, drawer, and cabinet, searching for images of the woman. Once, a mother had hidden photographs of herself all over her house, behind loose wallpaper and affixed to the undersides of chairs, desperate that if she went, some image of her should remain; a selfish action, painful for her husband and confounding for her children. The fathers were much more careful now. When they had gathered up everything, the pictures of her from albums and from frames on tables and hanging on walls, they carried them out and threw them into a great pile on the lawn. Little children liked to help. They stepped to the edge of the pile and sprinkled on twigs and dead white leaves. We lit the fire. Like I said, it was a damp and windless day, and the fire smoldered and burned without sparks. As I always did, I picked out one of the images in the pile to watch. This time it was a picture of the woman beaming as she sat in a rocking chair, hand on her round belly, a silver chain with a crystal pendant around her neck. I watched and waited for the moment I loved best, that split second between when a picture caught and when it was consumed, when the image appeared to travel backward and became again the negative of itself. The crystal pendant turned black. The woman's smiling mouth became a white void.

Smoke tendriled into the sky like vines climbing the air, and when it reached the clouds it joined them. She was truly gone now. The clouds held her, as they held all our gone mothers, and at night when we opened our windows and invited the clouds in, they would enter us: memories we could not touch, a feeling we could not name.

I became aware then of some commotion at the front. The little boy had leaped down from the porch rail and was pushing through the crowd in his underclothes and boots, wielding his elbows to force us to make way. When he reached the fire, he fell to his knees beside it and thrust his hands into the smoldering embers, grabbing at what were by then only the ashes of his mother's image. A father was on him almost immediately, pulling him away. Such episodes were not uncommon; we were ready for them. The boy flailed in the father's arms. He kicked and pummeled and screamed. We couldn't look away, his body so small, his pain so exquisite.

It was then I spotted Ruth at the edge of the crowd. She wore the dress with the white flowers. She clasped her hands at her chest and kneaded her fingers together. She would begin to understand it now, the beauty and brutality of our lives. Her gaze shifted away from the commotion and turned in my direction, picking me out of the crowd. I gave her a slight, solemn smile. I wanted to go over and tell her how happy we were she was here, but she didn't return my smile, and I realized she wasn't quite looking at me, but slightly past me, at my father. Then the boy let out a moan, like the labor sounds that came from the clinic where our mothers birthed, and Ruth and my father looked away from each other, back to the front. It had taken three fathers to subdue the boy. He lay curled in the grass, his limbs and face and the undershirt smudged with ash, his hands, red and raw, held away from his body, fingers curled. A father tried to stroke his hair, and at first the boy jerked away from his touch. Then he let his body go limp and acquiesced. When I looked back at the spot where Ruth had been, she was gone.

That afternoon, Di, Marie, and I went to the Op Shop to look at the new items on offer. It was crowded, girls and women cheek by jowl sorting through it all, plucking good finds from one another's grasp: a pair of loafers, barely broken in; a brassiere with fine lace edging; perfume in a violet bottle. Marie found a white blouse with a stiff collar; it had a small stain on the lapel, but she was 'certain a little bicarbonate of soda' would 'get that right out.' Di purchased a pair of blue twill pants that hugged her curves. I didn't even bother looking through the clothes, which would be too big for me. My size was almost always a barrier on these days. I had just parted ways with Di and Marie on the sidewalk when I ran into Ruth.

'It's a good haul today,' I said cheerfully.

'I'm not going in.'

I had never heard her speak in such a sharp tone, and it stung, though I knew it wasn't personal. The day's events had to have been a shock for her. She stroked the ribbon on her hat.

'I'm so happy you were with us this morning. We all are. It feels complete when you're here.' I spoke all in a rush, then stood breathless before her, aroused by the feelings I had expressed to her. I expected her to make some kind of reply, but she just stood there looking at me with an expression I couldn't quite figure out, fear or confusion or maybe disapproval. 'I know it's a lot to take in.'

'She's just gone then.' She put the fingers of one hand together, then opened them out.

I nodded.

'And you allow it to happen.'

'We don't allow anything. It isn't up to us.'

'But you live with it. You accept it.'

She could only see the horror of it. She couldn't see what we saw: Something happened here that happened no place else. We didn't know why it happened, or how. We didn't demand answers from it because our affliction itself had taught us that you cannot wrest answers from a mystery. We submitted to it. We bore it, carried it, so that there would be a place on this earth where people lived as we did and knew the things we knew. We did this not only for ourselves but also for them, for *her,* even if she could not appreciate it. We were necessary.

'You don't understand it yet, but you will,' I tried. 'You just need to be patient.'

I thought this would reassure her, but it only seemed to agitate her further.

'I've never seen you wear that necklace before,' she said.

I clutched the chain at my throat. 'I just bought it.'

'It was hers?'

I nodded. It had been an incredible find, hard to believe someone hadn't snatched it up before me, the necklace with the crystal pendant from the photograph, the silver chain so thin and fine it had pooled in the palm of my hand like liquid when I picked it up in the Op Shop.

'And you don't feel odd with it around your neck?'

'If you'd only go in and choose something and put it on, you might begin to feel it the way we do. It's a bit mad in there right now, but I could go with you. It wouldn't be any trouble.'

'No thank you,' she said tersely.

It was a terrible feeling to have Ruth be cross with me, even though if I was honest, I was also feeling less warmly toward her. For weeks, she had relished the beauty of our town and our lives here, but now she wasn't even attempting to understand. It seemed to me that something nasty she had been concealing was starting to slip out.

'There will be a recital tonight. You should come.' I had hoped since she arrived that she would get to see a recital, us as I loved us best. But even as I told her she should come, I no longer meant it quite the way I would have even five minutes before, and when she told me she would be there, I felt neither happy nor disappointed, only a sense that we had reached a standoff, which could not hold for long.

It was a beautiful night for a recital, cool and with breeze enough to keep the flying insects at bay, and in Feldpark, where we gathered on the grass around the fountain of the crying woman, the clouds were thick all around us. We claimed our spots. The ground was firm and cold, and we felt it through the blankets we laid out. When we brushed our hands against the grass, it left them wet, and we rubbed the wetness into our hair or wiped it against our legs. We spread out our picnics. Small children dozed off, heavy in our laps, unable to fight sleep long enough to hear the music; when the recital was over, we would carry them home in our arms, and when they woke in the morning and realized they had missed it, some of them would cry.

It was during this period before the music began that we turned and saw her, standing at the edge of the field. As she moved among us, we offered her bits of our picnics, fiddlehead salad, cold sliced beef, bread slathered with onion butter, spiced wafers wrapped in a lace napkin. Someone had thought to bring an extra blanket for her, and she accepted this and spread it on the grass.

We went up year by year, starting with the kinders. The little boy from the morning was among them. His eyes were puffy from crying, but he wore a dress shirt snugly tucked into his trousers and his hair was neatly combed. His hands were wrapped in white gauze that seemed to glow in the twilight. The kinders hadn't begun their instruments yet. They sang. We never had them perform simple pieces, or cute ones, but chants and rounds and songs in foreign tongues, and every year our youngest schoolchildren startled us with their feeling for the music. The boy with the wrapped hands had a solo. He sang with his eyes closed and his head uplifted. His voice trembled. He was so impossibly small, his loss so impossibly vast. Already, so early in the night, the recital was doing its work, making beauty of darkness.

After the kinders came the firsts with their recorders, playing their piercing, off-key notes. Up they went, seconds, thirds, fourths, fifths. I remembered being each of these ages. The pinch of my braids in kindergarten when Marie's mother redid my father's clumsy attempt. The cool wood of a recorder in my mouth. The fingerboard tape in primary colors on my violin's neck when I was just learning. The pieces we'd played and how it felt to be inside each one, and most of all the alchemy by which the labored plucking and blowing of twenty children became music, and memory. I ached with the knowledge that we uppers would never again be together in just this way. When it was finally our turn, I took my seat onstage with all the boys and girls I had never not known, and we began. At first it happened just like I wanted. My own bowing was consumed by the music we made together and it was beautiful, the most beautiful thing we knew. But something kept stopping me from losing myself in it the way I wanted to. My eyes kept landing on Ruth in the crowd. She speared a chunk of sliced beef. Licked onion butter from her shining lips. She rubbed a hand back and forth against the soft knit blanket. She closed her eyes to savor our music, and all the while our clouds caressed her skin. We lavished offerings of every kind upon her and she accepted them all. We loved her, we welcomed her, we accepted her with all of her limitations. But what did she give us in return?

I was awakened in the dead of night by strange noises, like the sounds of nocturnal animals in the forest. The sounds came from my father's

room. I pressed my ear to the thin wall that separated my room from
his and listened, and though I had never heard such sounds before, I
knew that this was lovemaking: the rhythmic knocking of the head-
board against the wall, my father's grunts, a woman's hitched breath,
faster and faster until all at once my father cried out in pain and the
woman released a moan of boundless pleasure.

After that, nothing, silence. Then footsteps, descending the stairs.
I went to my window and there she was, Ruth, going out our front
door, which we left so trustingly unlatched.

I knew it then, though it was painful to know. I had never been special
to our stranger. She had not trusted me as she did not trust others. She
had only ever been trying to win *my* trust, so that she could make her
way into our home and take from my father that greatest offering,
that highest pleasure. She must have laid her plans on her very first
day in town, when she came into Rapid and asked me, 'Just the two of
you?' I had thought only of my own embarrassment when I told her
it was; I hadn't for a moment considered that I might be providing
her just the information she sought, letting her know that my father
was alone. Did she even care about photography at all, or had that,
too, been part of her scheme? I had been so touched by the way she
made herself mild to match my father's mildness. How had I failed to
see this for what it was, the behavior of a woman who could change
herself at will, who would become whatever was necessary to extract
everything she could from us? I felt very foolish. All the stories we
knew of strangers, and still I had let myself fall for her deceptions.

The next afternoon during my break from my shift at Rapid, I went for
a walk. I made my way across town to Sally's kiosk, where I ordered a

cheese and chutney sandwich. As Sally melted lard on the griddle, she made small talk like she always did.

'Looks like our stranger will be staying around,' she said gleefully. 'You know, she adores my cheese and chutney. My ham and gherkin, too.'

Sally turned away from me and flipped the sandwich on the griddle.

'She came to our house last night,' I said. 'She took pleasure from my father. She's not what she would have us believe.'

It wasn't long before all of us had heard Sally's rumor, and the gossip in town was of little else. The stranger Ruth had insinuated herself into the bed of a man who, we all agreed, now that we had occasion to discuss it, was among the most abject of us all, not a person a woman would be drawn to if her intentions were pure. Rather, her act revealed a selfish hunger, and an indifference, even contempt, toward us in our particulars, that shocked us at first. But the more we considered it, the less shocked we became. It was as if Sally's rumor confirmed a truth about our stranger we must have always known, though we had not wanted to see it. We noticed things about her we hadn't at first, or maybe it would be more precise to say we began to see the things she did in a different light. The gifts, to start with. She had always tried to refuse them, and had accepted them only with great hesitation, as if she did not believe she deserved them, and this had endeared her to us, and convinced us she was not like other strangers, and made us eager to go on giving to her. But now it seemed to us that she had taken and taken. We were forced to consider the possibility that she had tricked us into handing her just what she wished to steal from us.

Then there were her daily sojourns into the mountains. We had been so happy that she was bearing witness to their beauty. But what if with these walks she was merely evading us to render herself less accessible, and therefore more desirable? We thought back to her vigilance the day she arrived, how she had struck us as vulnerable and afraid and our hearts had gone out to her; now we detected in that vigilance an indication of her meticulous efforts to mislead us.

We reminded ourselves that all of this was to be expected. She was a stranger, and she was what strangers always were: They saw our lives here, a beauty that was closed to them, and they could not be bothered to understand it; they could think only of what they wanted to take of it for themselves.

Now, when we saw her on a bench in Feldpark, we gave her a wide berth. When our children made her pictures or bracelets, we did not permit them to offer these gifts to her. We kept them close. Still, despite the mounting evidence against her, we held out some dwindling hope that we were mistaken, that it was all a big misunderstanding. Until, that is, a maid at the Alpina decided to dust the pile of gifts that had accumulated on the windowsill in the stranger's room. Among the drawings and carvings, the lanyards and liquors and sweets, concealed in the folds of the embroidered kerchief from Esther, she discovered a small object none of us had given to the stranger. A silver hairpin. The one thing which, for all our abundant generosity toward her, we would never offer her, because we couldn't; she wasn't one of us and wasn't meant to have it. A few days earlier we might have dismissed this theft as the behavior of a woman who could be no better than she was. We might have believed she had simply stolen an object whose beauty she could not resist, and assumed she had no notion of the significance of what she had taken. But we knew better now. This theft cast a pure bright light on the rumor Sally had shared with us, and in this light at last we saw the stranger Ruth's agenda with undeniable clarity.

We had always noticed the way she watched our mothers, but until then we had attributed her fixation to the painful contrast between their lives and her own. Now we saw plainly the rapaciousness leaching out from deep within the rigorous neutrality of her countenance, and we understood that her true desire was not to have what our mothers had, but to supplant us, to weave one of our pins into her foreign hair and with it to pierce one of our fathers; to stitch herself a suit from a mother's skin and to feast in that dark, wet interior.

The maid at the Alpina left a note on her pillow. *Go.* But she did not go. It seemed we would be forced to take matters into our own hands.

Because of these developments, I was surprised when Ruth came into Rapid during my shift. She wore her trousers and the chambray shirt, the sleeves rolled carelessly to her elbows. There were dark circles under her eyes, she looked unwell, and the sight of her in this state pleased me even as it turned my stomach. I resolved to be courteous, no more, no less.

'How may I help you?' I asked.

She removed a roll of film from her pocket and set it on the counter. 'I want this developed.' She spoke hastily, as if this were one of numerous errands she must complete this afternoon, though we both knew she had no responsibilities, nothing to do and nowhere to be.

'Just the one?' She had to have purchased ten rolls since she arrived.

'That's right.'

I had been hoping she would decide to have us develop her film ever since she made her first purchase on the day of her arrival, and now that she had, I was so disappointed that she had brought only this one roll. This only added to the evidence against her. What must be on the other rolls that she didn't want us to see? Pictures of us captured without our consent? Photographs of the objects she wished to purloin from us?

I swept the roll into the In basket. I thought she would go then, but she lingered uncertainly. She pressed her lips together and seemed to stare at a point on the wall behind me. Then she spoke. 'You could leave this place.'

It was the last thing I expected her to say, and for a moment I just stared at her. 'Why would I do that?'

'It could be your image they burn someday.'

She could never understand, I was coming to see, not if she lived among us a hundred years. And for the first time I did not feel the least bit sorry for her, but looked upon her with disgust.

'And what,' I said, 'is the biggest thing that could possibly happen to you?'

I stood there shocked by myself and what she had brought out of me. She summoned a pained, wounded expression, but I knew better now than to fall for it. 'This will be ready tomorrow.'

'Thank you,' she whispered, and went out of the shop.

I didn't think she would dare come to our house that night, but she did, and once more I lay awake listening to the sounds of her stolen pleasure.

We were in quite the bind then. She could not stay here, nor could we allow her to leave. We did not trust her with our secret elsewhere. When we gathered outside of the Alpina the next morning, we had not yet coalesced upon a plan. We understood only that some action was required. We peered in the windows of the dining room and watched as she ate her breakfast of yogurt and stewed fruit, drank her tea with milk and four cubes of sugar. When she finished, we assembled at the hotel's entrance. She must have seen us and understood what was happening, because she did not immediately come out, but went back up to her room. We waited patiently in place. When she finally emerged, she held the leather valise. She had changed her clothes, too. She was wearing what she'd worn the first day, the crepe dress with the small white flowers, the soft brown boots, the straw hat with the ribbons hanging loose over her hair, which was also loose; she hadn't bothered to braid it. She knew we knew the truth of her now, and there was no use continuing with her deceptions.

The maid from the Alpina approached her and grasped the valise, and the stranger let her lift it out of her hands. The maid laid it on the cobblestones, opened the clasps, and began to sift through the items stuffed haphazardly inside, her clothes and shoes, our gifts, the rolls of film. When she found what she was looking for, she stood and held it high in the air. The silver hairpin shone in the soft morning light.

'Thief,' the maid said.

Ruth made no attempt to deny this accusation.

A mother stepped forward and removed the rolls of film from the valise, collecting them in her basket. 'Can't have you taking these with you.' She closed the valise, fastened the clasps, and pressed it back into the stranger's hands.

We began to move as one. We pressed in on her until she was compelled to walk. We formed a sort of arrow, the stranger our tip, all of us fanning out behind her, and in this formation we pushed her through our streets. As we walked she looked around at our shops and houses, our gardens, the mountains, the scraps of the night's clouds that still lingered in the air, all the beauty she would never see again. On Berg-strasse she halted and turned to us.

'Please,' she begged.

It was a painful moment. How we wished she had been the woman we first took her to be, true and well-intentioned, in which case she could have stayed, we could have kept her forever. But she wasn't, we couldn't, and as she faced us, the truth of her predicament, and of her own role in it, seemed to come down on her.

We pressed on, past the statue of the crying woman in Feldpark, across the dew-soaked grass, into the forest, through the skinfruit grove and the dense thickets where the goats fed, until we reached the Graubach. I had started out somewhere near the back of the pro-cession, but by that point I had made my way to the very tip of it. I belonged there, on account of how she had preyed especially upon me and my father, who even now was too reticent to do anything but stand at the back of the crowd, eyes on the ground.

We were massed between the embankment and the river's edge, water lapping at our feet. The mother who had gathered the film in her basket stepped forward and tossed the rolls one by one into the river. The water was unusually high that day and it carried them swiftly away.

Like I said, we did not have a clear plan for our stranger. There was a peculiar sort of pause then, and I think we all, she and we alike, felt the weight of the impasse we had reached: how badly we had wanted things to work out differently, how far too late it was for any correc-tions. Ruth's gaze darted from face to face, unfocused, her expression unreadable as always, whether desperate or angry, full of envy or re-vulsion. It was then her eyes landed on me.

'Vera!' she cried. 'Please.'

Some part of me still craved her, still cracked at the sound of my name in her mouth. But I kept my wits about me. I stepped toward her. I clasped her hand in both of mine. I could feel it trembling, like a baby bird trembles, and I saw the hope in her eyes. I grasped my gold bangle with the red stones, slipped it off her wrist, and returned it to my own. 'We don't want a stranger here,' I said. 'We already have everything we need.'

I pressed closer to her and the rest of us followed me. This movement I had started forced her to walk a few paces deeper into the river. Still, the water was only up to her knees, barely nipping at the hem of her dress. But the green rocks below her must have been especially slick, and on one of these she slipped. She made the smallest sound. A yelp, more of surprise than anything. A moment later the river had pulled her to its center, where the current was strongest, and swept her downstream. Within seconds she was gone, carried off beyond our borders to where we could not follow. Only her straw hat remained, bobbing slowly in her wake, the black ribbons floating on the water's surface. Did she swim? Did she drown? It was beyond our control.

II

School ended and we uppers began sifting out into couples. We knew this next stage of our lives was coming, had been waiting for it forever; still, we, or at least I, was surprised by how quickly it happened. Already at the next supply, several girls from our year were placing special orders for perfume and lace trim to sew onto their underthings, and boys were ordering gifts that were particular to these girls: a set of oil paints, wood stretchers, and a roll of canvas for one; a flower press for another to preserve the specimens she liked to collect.

At that supply my father and I were in line behind Sally. When it was her turn, she couldn't resist sharing with Mr. Phillips that we'd had a stranger in town, and that she had been the first to see her. 'I sensed right away she wasn't to be trusted,' Sally now claimed.

Mr. Phillips pursed his lips. 'I'm sorry to hear it.'

'Oh, we don't hold it against *you*.' She reached out a hand and placed it atop Mr. Phillips's on the table. I cringed, but Mr. Phillips was polite enough to let her hand rest there a moment before sliding his out from underneath.

'This stranger, is she in a position to cause you any further trouble?' he asked.

'I should think not,' Sally said, arms crossed proudly over her chest, as if this was all thanks to her.

Mr. Phillips nodded slowly. Sally stood there, eyes gleaming, desperate to be asked more questions, but he said nothing further. Sally was such an embarrassment, thinking our stranger would be of interest to Mr. Phillips, who lived his whole life elsewhere among strangers. Still, when Sally finished placing her requests and it was our turn, I couldn't resist holding out my wrist, on which I wore my gold bangle, and telling him how the stranger had tricked me into offering it to her.

'But I got it back just in time. I was right at the front at the end.'

'How fortunate,' Mr. Phillips said, though it seemed to me he spoke rather pityingly, like he thought I was no better than Sally. I was so mortified that I found myself quite spontaneously adding a lip salve I'd heard girls talking about to our order. It was supposed to soften your lips for when you kissed. I had no boy to use it for, but I didn't want Mr. Phillips to know it.

By the time he returned for the next supply, with the lace trim and my gratuitous salve and all the rest, Ana and Jonathan were a couple. At night when I looked out my bedroom window I would see them together, his hands in her hair, lips to her neck. A few years later, they became the first of us to marry. The coupling of Ana and Jonathan was a shock. We would have expected her to select someone with a dominance and confidence to match her own. Jonathan was considered something of an odd bird. He kept mostly to himself. He trapped and hunted animals in the forest, rabbits and deer and old doe goats that had stopped producing milk, and sold the carcasses to the butcher, the pelts to the proprietor of the leather goods shop. Much as I wanted to think Ana was rushing things, hurrying into any match just to be first, as soon as I started seeing them around together, I couldn't deny her vision in choosing him. It was such a tricky balance, finding the right match: We wanted someone who would draw out of us whatever peril we carried. We wanted to inhabit the full body of our affliction, to feel all the inches of its power and our vulnerability to it. But we also wanted to be spared. We sought a partner who would watch us as we approached the edge, and who would know the exact right moment to pull us back from it. Once, just after their wedding, I passed the house Ana and Jonathan now shared on Gartenstrasse and I saw them together in the yard. Ana watched as Jonathan slipped the hide from a deer's silvery carcass, his hands working gently, yet with a queer indifference, over the body of the animal, Ana's eyes transfixed and unblinking as the deer's black eyes. Within the year Ana had given birth to a daughter, Teresa.

Other girls quickly followed. Esther and Lu were close behind, their threesome had coordinated, as threesomes often did, and their babies were born within a six-month span. Di married a boy from the year above ours, and had her twins, a boy and a girl born early and small, eyes sealed shut like kittens, and I watched a new woman step out from the Di I had always known, or thought I had, one with dark circles beneath her eyes she did not bother to cover with powder, who nursed both children at once on a bench in Feldpark and didn't try to conceal her breasts, which were riven with shadowy blue veins. Not long after that, Marie wed a man several years older than us whose first wife had gone when their child was an infant, and Marie fell into mothering the baby effortlessly, like this task, this life, had been waiting for her all along.

During this period, I worked at Rapid full-time, though there was little for me to do beyond being the counter girl any shop requires. Girls from my year came into Rapid regularly now to develop pictures of their weddings and their honeymoons in the suite at the Alpina: the four-poster bed with the rosette coverlet, the dish of chocolate-covered berries glistening with condensation on a wing table, the braided rug before the stone hearth. Mothers came to develop pictures of their babies, as they always had, but now they were girls I had grown up with, girls no longer. All around me girls were beginning to slip into their fates, and I feared that I, too, had slipped into mine: to live and work and sleep alongside a father instead of a husband, separated by the thin walls between the darkroom and the front of the shop, his bedroom and mine; to watch him grow old; to care for him and someday to bury him and then, no longer young myself, to assume his position in the darkroom and to grow old alone in that small, dark space, an old woman who was still a child because her life had taught her none of what a mother knows.

I saw the mothers everywhere. Di and her husband walking hand in hand through town, one of the twins wrapped to each of their chests. Meek Rachel from our year, pregnant in front of me in line at the bakery, making a joke about eating for two and complimenting me on my figure, how thin I'd stayed since school, her hand resting protectively on her belly the whole time. Ana, Esther, and Lu pushing their prams around Feldpark, lips stained red from skinfruit.

I watched these girls, now mothers, parading their babies about town and taking roll upon roll of photographs of them, as if there were nothing you could do to use them up, and I consoled myself with the bitterest thought: *You could be torn from this child.* I thought how careless of them, how indulgent, to let their children out of their bodies, while I kept mine secreted away inside me, deprived myself of them to keep them safe.

But in the end, I did marry. I was not even especially late to do so. Peter was in my year but we had never been friends. We were both fairly shy and hewed closely to the comfort of our groups. It was a toothache, of all things, that brought us together. Peter's father had always been our town's dentist, and he had recently finished training Peter to take over. I came in with a sore molar, and Peter, in his white coat over a dress shirt and trousers, led me down the corridor to the examination room and gestured rather sheepishly to the beige chair. I reclined, supine beneath his gaze.

'Open wide, please.'

He lifted his implements from a cloth on a small table and brought them into my mouth. His fingertips grazed my cheek lightly. The metal implements clinked against my teeth.

It turned out to be nothing serious. He prepared a poultice for me to apply twice a day after rinsing with salt water. He walked me to the door, and I was about to leave when he mentioned that he had no other patients until the afternoon and asked if I might like to go for a walk. From then on, we often walked together in the late mornings, when business was slow for us both. In the beginning, we meandered, neither of us assertive enough to want to determine the route, but soon we had settled into 'our loop': Hauptstrasse to Bergstrasse, then through the trees to the Graubach, where we liked to sit on the bank with our feet in the water, wiggling our toes incrementally nearer to each other until they touched, returning to town via a quiet backstreet called Hinter der Wald. When I told Peter it was my favorite street, I loved its overgrown gardens and the way the forest seemed to wrap itself around the houses, he said it was his, too, and we grew a bit shy then; we both understood we had confessed something significant and personal to each other.

One day on our walk, as we made our way through the forest to the river, we heard a rustling in the undergrowth. Peter put his arm out in front of me protectively, and we watched a red fox slip out from the bushes and patter off. The next day when Peter met me outside of Rapid for our loop, he handed me a small white box. Inside was a carving of a fox, fine and delicate, a few curled shavings still clinging to it. 'My hand slipped, just there,' he said, pointing to a groove in the wood and shrugging good-naturedly. I kept the fox under my pillow. At night I took it out and stroked the smooth wood, rubbed it against my cheek, my neck, slipped my fingernail into the groove.

Our bond deepened quickly. It felt less like we were building something, stone upon stone, than like we were uncovering it, a structure hidden in the forest, pulling away the moss and ferns to find what had been waiting there. In truth, I had never given Peter much consideration before. At school he had been well-liked though not at all prominent, diligent enough with his cello and his studies but with no notable talent in any particular direction. All I had really known about him was that he was the dentist's son and he wanted, or perhaps simply expected, to become a dentist himself. Yet it was now these very qualities, Peter's temperate and guileless nature, the translucence of his inner life, that drew me to him. It seemed a kind of miracle that a person should exist this way, as if it were no burden at all to be just who he was.

Not long after we began our courtship, a mother went. At the burning, he sought me out in the crowd.

'Did you know her well?'

I shook my head. 'I never even spoke to her.'

'Still.' He took my hand in his. It was our first time holding hands, and he had chosen this moment for it, here, as the fire snapped and the smoke rose and the mothers whispered. He didn't hold my hand in the gentle way I expected, but firmly, as if it required a forceful grip to keep it from slipping away. I saw then that he was drawn not just to me, but also to the dark potential all women in our town carried inside us, and I was startled to realize he feared me a little. I began to know what women here had always known: We were endangered, but we were dangerous, too; our peril was also our power.

We had sex for the first time a few weeks later. I had come over to Peter's house for dinner, as I had begun doing regularly. Peter was the eldest of three brothers. His mother cooked like her husband and sons were woodsmen instead of dentists and schoolboys, roasts and casseroles and curries with rice so buttery it glistened. The boys played pranks on one another, left thorns on seat cushions, snuck red pepper into one another's food, and their mother scolded them even as she laughed, each of them the apple of her eye. There was never a quiet moment at the table, they all talked and talked. Nothing especially interesting or clever, just ordinary things: anecdotes from the day, upcoming plans, household tasks and repairs and how they planned to complete them. I had always thought Peter was quiet like me, but he wasn't quiet here, in this family life with its effortless operations. I tried not to think then of my father, alone in our silent house.

After dinner, Peter led me upstairs to his room and we slid together into his bed. I was so nervous. I had no experience whatsoever. He smelled of sweet sweat where his curls met the nape of his neck, and of the pink soap with which he washed his hands between patients. Pulling down his pants released a musk I would search out on my fingers for hours that night after I got home, unable to sleep. Over all of this was the perfume of detergent on his sheets. I knew that his mother had washed them for him, and made this bed. Peter had never not had her smoothing the way for him, whispering lovingly in his ear, and the scent of the detergent fueled my desire almost as much as Peter himself. When he entered me, I removed my silver hairpin from my braid; I knew at least that much about what to do. As he moved over me, I pricked his shoulder with the tine and placed my mouth over the welling blood. I tasted everything in it, black dirt of the forest, shallow green water at the river's edge, the tang of Peter's metal implements in my mouth.

All the next day, whenever my fingertips brushed against someone else's, handing change to a customer, purchasing a slice of tea cake at the bakery, lending my salve to Marie, all the touches of my day sent a shiver through me; they were Peter's touches, too, freighted with our lovemaking. That afternoon, when we slipped away to a secluded spot in the forest, amid the churring of insects, the screams of creatures in the trees, faint trembling of goats moving in packs through the undergrowth, his hands on me were all of our hands. I had tasted his blood and it was all in me now: him, here, *us*.

Our wedding was a wonderful party. We were all there, Di and Marie with their husbands and children, Peter's friends, even Ana, Esther, and Lu; we always invited the others from our school year to our weddings. We danced all night, Peter and I right at the center of it all, his parents kicking off their shoes, his brothers cutting in to take turns with me, Ana squatting low despite her round belly, full with her second child, to dance with little Teresa, allowing herself to enjoy the night even if it was my wedding. Meanwhile, my father sat alone at a table at the edge of the dancing. He wore the same suit he'd worn to marry my mother. He hadn't gained a pound in all these years; his body had undergone the transition from youth to age without altering its dimensions. Every so often I glanced over at him. He sifted absently through confetti, sipped from his glass, rolled his sleeves up then down again. I knew I should go to him, be with him, but I didn't. After all, it was my wedding, I never wanted to leave the dance floor. At some point I looked back and he was gone. He had slipped out without even saying goodbye; he wouldn't ever want to interrupt. How it shamed me: the silent life we had shared, how insufficient it had been and how I had loved it, and was now leaving it, and him, behind.

After the party, Peter and I made our way to the Alpina for our time in the honeymoon suite. I had seen the suite countless times in photos. Now here I was, here it was: the four-poster bed with the rosette coverlet, the braided rug in front of the stone hearth, the chocolate-covered berries on the wing table, their glossy exteriors clouded with condensation. Last week it had been Susanna and the month before it had been Klara, and before that Marie, Di, Lu, Esther, Ana. My mother and father had slept in this room, and made love in it. Now it was my turn, my wedding dress tossed over the brocade chair, my knees burning as I knelt before my husband on the braided rug that knew all our knees. It had been them and now it was me. I could have been any of us.

We moved into a beautiful house on Hinter der Wald. It had a gabled roof with wide eaves, a front porch lined with handsome balusters, windows trimmed with carvings of stars. Its only shortcoming was its location directly across the street from Sally's house. We had been living there less than a year when Ana's youngest brother knocked on our door one morning, panting, having sprinted all the way from Eschen, and told me to come quickly. By the time I arrived it was too late. My father was gone. His heart, most likely; he had collapsed on the sidewalk when he was setting out for Rapid.

For days Peter and I were never without guests and their offerings, pies and casseroles and jars of berry jam, which I spread on toast but could not eat because of how it quivered. Sally was one of the first to arrive, with a fricassee in her arms, her hair in sausage curls for the occasion. She showed herself to the kitchen and set the fricassee on the counter, then came to me in the parlor and gathered me in an embrace so tight I could smell the powder on her breasts. It was just like Sally, this showy display, which suggested a much more intimate relationship between us than actually existed, so that she might stake some claim to this drama. 'I'm so sorry, my dear,' she said. 'So good you have something to look forward to.' She placed a hand on my belly, and I allowed this though the feeling of her hand there, so near, set off a ferocious possessiveness in me. I was six months along. We'd had no trouble at all. I didn't even have morning sickness. Marie was always saying how lucky I was. We were pregnant at the same time, she was two months ahead. She and her husband had tried for years, and when it finally happened, the smell of beans on the stove was enough to make her ill. Meanwhile, I craved just the foods an unborn baby was said to require, yams and peas and wild greens. Peter was forever running to the butcher to fetch liver for me, and even when he unwrapped the brown waxed paper to reveal it, gleaming slabs the dark red of the stones in my bangle, I didn't feel ill, felt only appetite. He soaked the liver in milk then fried it in butter, making sure to crisp the edges as I liked. He doted on me, on us, as husbands did, subordinating themselves to wives and the burdens we bore, eager to meet every want, sooth every discomfort, so that we might be free to let motherhood bring out only the best in us.

I tried to accept Marie's verdict that I was lucky, that my body, which seemed to know just what to do, and to be so at ease in pregnancy, was a positive sign. But it was not so simple. At night, my mind conjured the most terrible dreams. In one, the creature growing inside me wasn't a baby at all, but a shrunken little adult. Somehow I knew that its face, wizened like an old skinfruit, was my mother's face. She had been waiting inside me all this time, and now she had stolen my baby's body, and I would give birth to her. In another, the baby was born perfect, smooth-skinned and lovely as a porcelain doll. I took my child everywhere. But then I looked in the pram, and in place of the beautiful child was filthy, desecrated Walina. My baby had never been real, had only ever been a figment of my desire. It was Walina I'd carried around all this time, while the rest of us looked on in horror.

I shared these dreams with Peter, and discussed with him the anxieties of which they were so clearly an indication.

'Do you think I'll be a good mother?' I must have asked him this a thousand times.

'Are you kidding? You'll be wonderful. You're patient. You're resilient. You're kind.' He was right, I was these things, I didn't doubt it. Yet I suspected that being a good mother had little to do with possessing those traits good mothers ought to possess, that it hinged on something else entirely, required other, obscure qualities that could be neither honed nor harnessed.

How does a motherless mother *mother*? How does she know how, or does she simply not know? And if she doesn't, can she learn it on her own, or can she never learn it because she didn't have a mother to teach her? I reminded myself it wasn't true I was motherless. Many nights as my child grew inside me, I lay awake, resisting sleep and the dreams sleep brought, and chased the tails of my earliest memories, trying to catch my mother in them. I remembered standing on the riverbank after we shot down the seabird and watching the father hold it under the water. I felt a weight in the memory, a pull, and I knew it was my mother, standing beside me on the bank. But when I tried to turn away from the bird and look at her, see her, I lost the memory, as if it sensed what I was up to and expulsed me.

I remembered the morning after she went. The sight of everyone massed in our yard. I turned away from them. I buried my face in my father's chest and wailed. I could remember the feeling of my grief in that moment, my need to be soothed by the one person who wasn't there, the dawning understanding that she never would be, not ever again. But when I tried to get the memory to give up more, to show me the mother I longed for in that moment, it denied me and denied me. I could see the burning, smell the heavy smoldering of wet wood and see the smoke rise into the clouds until I couldn't tell where it ended and they began. But I could not see the images we burned, of which the smoke was made.

Still, I had to believe her mothering was in me, hidden away somewhere too deep for me to access, but which might still serve me with my own child. Only here I ran up against an unanswerable question. My mother had not loved as other mothers loved; her going was all the proof I needed of this. Impossible to say, whether what traces of her I carried would guide me, or lead me astray.

Peter and I decided to close Rapid. With my father gone, I was the only one in town who could manage the darkroom, and I was soon to have my hands full. At first Peter suggested I train someone, so that they could keep the shop going until I was ready to return. Sweet Peter, he would never suggest that we do the obvious thing and rid ourselves of the store. It sold quickly, to Esther's husband, Nicolas. He had no interest in buying the business. He planned to put in a sporting goods store. From then on, our town no longer had a photo shop. If you wanted a camera or film, you had to special order from Mr. Phillips, and when you wanted the film developed he took it to a shop in the city, and we were very careful from then on with what we photographed. People came up to me all the time and said how much they missed the old days when they could get their photos within the week and didn't feel the need to be so cautious. Peter and I did salvage a few useful things from the store. Albums which we would fill with family photos in the years to come. The wood table from the darkroom, which had held the developing trays over which my father labored all his silent years, and which was just the right height for a changing table.

There was little in my father's house worth keeping. His clothes we bagged and brought to the Op Shop. Furniture and knickknacks Peter and his brothers carried out to the sidewalk, free for the taking. Much else I disposed of, nobody would want it: my father's shaving kit; his pantry items, jars of spices so old they had turned colorless. I filled a single box with keepsakes. Walina, her cotton torso speckled with faded brown dots of blood. My father's comb, which I could not bring myself to throw away because it held the oils from his scalp, a yellow accumulation at the base of the tines. The wedding band he had never taken off. I held this a long time before packing it away. I thought of my father standing in my bedroom doorway all the evenings of my youth to say good night, his hand tapping rhythmically against the jamb, the ring making its own dull knock as it hit the wood. How tenderly he patted the jamb, as if he hoped to transmit his love through the wood to me. He had never been able to offer it to me directly, had given me only this meager token, a hand knocking wood when I longed to be patted to sleep, to hear him say, *I love you, Vera.*

I had never had this and now I never would; I would have to live my life without it.

Before I went out of the house, I took with me just one more thing. From beneath a loose floorboard in my childhood bedroom, I removed a slender Rapid Ready envelope. When the stranger Ruth slipped in the Graubach and was carried off by it, the roll of film she had brought to Rapid still sat untouched in the basket. Once she was gone, I had waited to see what my father would do with the film, but he did nothing; it sat there day after day. After a week of waiting, I could stand it no longer. One night I forced myself to stay awake until the whole town was asleep. I crept down the stairs, took my father's key ring from the pocket of his coat, and slipped out onto the street. I had never been out like this before, alone at night, when the clouds were fully settled over us, and I knew I shouldn't be, though as with most things we knew better than to do, we had no rule against it; a rule wasn't necessary, the clouds did all the work of one, keeping us to our houses. They were so dense I had to travel the route from home to Rapid by memory and touch, and as I hurried along I felt them wicking over my eyes, seeping between the strands of hair in my braid. I began to fear that I was giving the clouds too much of myself, letting them know me too well, but I couldn't resist the pull of Ruth's film, waiting so patiently for me in the basket, and anyway, once I unlocked the door to Rapid and stepped inside, I felt better. I snatched the roll, shut myself in the darkroom, and got to work: film onto reel, reel onto spindle, spindle into tank. *Agitate, invert, tap. Agitate, invert, tap.* When the negatives were ready, I clipped them to the line to dry, but of course I couldn't wait to print them to see what they contained. I was certain her photographs would hold traces of her dark intentions, evidence of the true nature it had taken us so long to detect. But the images were a disappointment, as the stranger herself had been; I could tell this even from viewing the small negatives in the red glow of the safelight. They couldn't have been more pedestrian. A trite close-up of flowers, their petals studded with dewdrops. The view from her window at the Alpina, rooftops piercing the clouds. The shops along Hauptstrasse. They were taken dead-on, no unexpected angles, each subject planted in the lifeless center of the composition. She had asked my father so many questions, but her photographs showed no indication she'd listened to a word he'd said. Her 'interest' in photography had been a sham like everything else about her, a ploy to seduce my father, for which we had fallen.

But when I came to the final negative, from the first photograph on the roll, there was something different about it, something I couldn't find the words to describe; my mind seemed to empty out at the sight of it. I squinted at it, trying to force it into a coherent shape, to locate the image in my mind, but it resisted. When the negatives were finally dry, I threaded this one into the enlarger before any of the others. It was just a blur at first, dark forms and light forms, and I turned the dial to bring it into focus, but even with the lines clear and sharp, I couldn't quite believe what I was seeing; the image seemed a kind of glitch, a trick, and I hurried the paper to the developer to confirm it. There it was, darkening the white paper: a vanished moment from a place that was no place I had ever seen. Ruth must have purchased this roll of film before she came to us and taken this single shot before her arrival. It had been taken on a balcony. In the foreground was a railing consisting of ornate curlicues in black metalwork, upon which an unfamiliar soot-gray bird roosted. In the background, several stories below, was a sort of large, open space surrounded by buildings, the ground paved in smooth gray stones. This space was nearly empty, just a few people scattered about, and the sky arced above it, a gray dome, as if carved from the same stone. This was elsewhere, stark and desolate, its people nothing but dark etches on a vast plane.

I snatched the other negatives from the drying line, crumpled them and hid them at the bottom of the waste bin. I tucked the photograph under my shirt and hurried back through the clouds to Eschen. I knew I should burn this picture. I should toss it in the Graubach. Instead, I had slipped it beneath the loose floorboard under my bed. I never took it out. It was not supposed to be here, and at night just the feeling of it there beneath me had a danger to it. Many times I thought I would throw it away, but I could never bring myself to. Now, I tucked it into the bottom of the box of keepsakes. Back at our home on Hinter der Wald, I pushed the box to the back of the top shelf of the hall closet. I didn't worry that Peter would find it because I had no such worries with Peter, who wasn't one to pry.

I had been married less than a year. My father was dead. Rapid was gone; you could buy rackets and cleats in what was once the darkroom. I would be a mother any day.

When the time came, I paced our house through the night. I released blood and mucus and clots of glistening black jelly into the toilet, vomited a thin green slime with every contraction. Peter wiped my mouth with a damp cloth, pressed his hands into my back with all his strength. At dawn we went to the clinic. In the birthing room I labored in the bed we all labored in, and where all of us and all of our children were born. It went on for hours that were lifetimes and no time at all, pain so unbearable it seemed impossible that every mother I knew had borne it, that every person I knew had been born. Peter coached me as he had been taught by the fathers in town. He squeezed my hand and said 'You can do this,' and 'Almost there,' and 'Yes, good, *push.*' Ordinary words, so insufficient to this task, the secret side of it he could not access, where it felt that my purpose was not to push this baby out but to pull myself in, to squeeze myself inside myself and join my child there. And yet it was also Peter's ordinary and insufficient encouragements, his faith that they were enough, that kept me going, and as the day lightened, our child left me and entered the world: a small, squalling gray thing, hair and skin coated in creamy white curds. The very moment the nurse laid my baby on my chest, I felt the childless, alone Vera I had always feared I would be burn away like clouds at midday. The baby was a girl. We named her Iris.

Our first afternoon home from the clinic, we were a bit at loose ends, uncertain what we were supposed to be doing. In the end we did nothing. I lay on the sofa in the parlor and Peter sat beside me with my feet in his lap; my feet had been cold the whole time we were at the clinic and now, at last, they were warm. Iris slept on my stomach, which was still so round. Peter and I watched as she rose and fell with my breath, and we marveled: at her improbable tininess, at her cheeks and forehead dusted with a pale shimmering fur, feet flaking gossamer skin, mouth suckling at the air even in sleep, pearly eyelids inlaid with whisper-thin red veins, the eyes beneath the shale color of the Graubach at its depths. After a while Peter dozed off, and I savored the feeling of lying awake in a room where the two dearest people to me in the world slept, utterly peaceful and vulnerable. When Iris woke, she nursed. Her soft wet mouth suckled with more force than I could have imagined such a small thing capable of exerting. I looked at this tiny creature at my breast, wholly dependent upon me, pure innocence. How could it be that she carried the potential to make me go, or to go

herself one day? For the first time, I felt the full weight of our affliction: the peril of immense loss and the power of immense love, the two
forces impossible to disentangle, for they were one and the same.

I was still nursing when we heard a knock at the door. Peter went to
open it, and there was Sally with a fricassee in her arms. Always, Sally
with her fricassees, for life's endings and its beginnings. She stood in
our doorway, peering past Peter into the parlor, where I sat hunched
uncertainly over Iris at my breast because I still had no notion what I
was doing.

'How thoughtful,' Peter said. 'Here, let me take that from you.'

Sally shook her head. 'Piping hot.' She wore oven mitts, no choice
but to invite her in to set the dish down. It was only once she was inside
that I noticed the camera around her neck and realized she was here
to take pictures of Iris. Sally had ordered an instant camera from Mr.
Phillips after Rapid closed. Now she always came to the homes of new
mothers so that they could have some early images of their babies while
they waited the time it took to give film to Mr. Phillips and for him to
return with the prints. Sally was a sort of genius about herself, able to
devise the most brilliant schemes for rendering herself indispensable at
significant moments so as to draw herself closer to the dramas of our
town, which never involved her directly. The instant camera allowed
her to offer a service for which new mothers were genuinely grate-
ful while granting her early access to them so that she could serve as
an authority on their acclimation to motherhood. I well remembered
the time, a year earlier, when a mother went and at the burning Sally
told everyone that she'd been expecting it ever since she took the newborn photos. She spoke without even an attempt at sobriety, unable to
contain her glee at possessing such valuable intelligence. According to

Sally, the way the mother looked at her baby had set her intuition clanging. When asked what, specifically, she had noticed, Sally would say only, with an air of great import, 'I know it when I see it.'

Despite all of this, like any new parents we wanted the photos, so we posed for Sally. Iris swaddled in my arms. Iris in her cradle, body curled like it was still in the womb. The three of us snuggled together on the sofa, Peter and I laughing because Iris had sneezed, the cutest thing we'd ever seen.

When Sally was done taking the photographs, she marched up to me. 'Come here, sweet girl,' she said, and without asking, she lifted Iris out of my arms. I let her do this. At first, I was too shocked to protest; then I wanted to rip Iris back from her, but I didn't dare, because it would only give Sally fodder. I looked at Peter, imploring him silently to intercede, but he was too polite to do such a thing. I expected Sally to hold Iris with great fanfare, maybe even to ask one of us to take a picture of her, but she didn't. Rather, with Iris cradled in her arms, she seemed to lose all awareness of Peter and me and her surroundings. Iris melted into Sally, and Sally into her. *Enough*, I wanted to say. *Give her back*. But I held my tongue. After quite some time, Sally looked up suddenly, as if startled from a reverie. She looked at me. 'Nobody can ever take this from you,' she said. She passed Iris back to me, and not long after that she said goodbye, advising me on her way out that while she knew to keep her visit brief, others might not be so considerate, and I must be sure 'not to let anyone overstay their welcome.' It was only once she was gone that I regained the composure to really consider what she had said earlier. Was she merely expressing her envy, because I had what she never would? Or was she implying something else, that she detected something in me? That on this day of my greatest happiness, I looked precarious to her?

'Forget Sally,' Peter said. 'I'm sure she uses that line on all the new moms to work you up.' He turned out to be right. A week later when I attended the new mom group for the first time, I would mention that Sally had invited herself in shortly after we returned home from the clinic, and the other mothers would jump in with their Sally stories, the way she'd all but snatched their babies out of their arms and the unnerving things she'd felt it necessary to say.

That night, we warmed Sally's fricassee in the oven. Peter moved Iris's cradle into the kitchen so we could tend to her while we ate. He had carved the cradle himself, the wood planed milk-smooth like the fox I now kept on my vanity in our bedroom. How I loved the sight of her in it, held so snug and safe, as if Peter were cradling her in his own hands. The meat in the fricassee was dark and wild, the sauce rich with wine and butter. My milk was just coming in. My breasts were heavy and swollen, throbbing as I had only known one part of my body to throb before. Never had I craved food more in my life and never had a food met that craving so exactly. I ate as if I would never be full.

The new mom group met in Feldpark every Tuesday at ten in the morning. That makes it sound very official, but it wasn't. It wasn't administered by anyone and attendance was by no means required, though pretty much all the new moms did attend, because it was so useful. The only one of us who never came was Ana. She had her third right around the time Iris was born. She didn't need group. She had 'three under three'; she was a pro. Nobody could remember when or how the group had formed, we all simply knew the field was reserved at ten on Tuesdays, just as the eleven o'clock hour was aerobics, so that as we new moms packed up our things and wrapped our babies against our chests, our town's women of late-middle-age swarmed in and rolled out their mats on the grass all around us, a source of mutual consternation: they thought we lingered, while we thought them sticklers about the hour, baffled they couldn't remember how difficult the newborn stage was. I tried to remind myself that their life stage possessed its own difficulties. While we young mothers were surveilled and scrutinized, these older women went all but unnoticed. They had managed to pass through their period of greatest vulnerability safely and had arrived on the other side of it only to find that now nobody cared about them or what they did.

We sat in a circle in the grass, our babies on blankets in front of us. We talked about nursing, diapering, soothing. It was through the examples of mothers a few months ahead of me at group that I learned the little maneuvers mothers know. How to nurse discreetly, unclasping my bra, hitching my shirt and unveiling my breast for a brief flash before the nipple disappeared into Iris's latch. How to stop caring so much about discretion, too, to leave my breast out after Iris came away, and to sling her over my shoulder and burp her before clasping my bra. How to burp her. The force with which the other mothers slapped their babies' backs! I hadn't known I was supposed to do it like this, had been patting Iris gently for minutes on end, desperate to coax out a burp; I fretted over hurting her, while the other mothers pounded their babies unconcerned. They seemed to take it as an article of faith that they could not harm them, that they knew instinctively how much force it was safe to levy upon their children. Marie was especially full of useful advice, little tips and tricks. Her pragmatism, her bland unimaginative nature, transformed now from vaguely annoying qualities into powers that allowed her to sail through the adjustment to motherhood.

I looked forward to these meetings desperately. I found myself keeping a running mental list of questions, anecdotes, things I wanted to discuss. I think the other mothers likely did the same. We saved this talk for one another, let it pour out so our husbands didn't have to hear it and know how tedious we had become.

Even more than we talked about the practicalities of motherhood, we discussed our reactions to it, searching out our commonalities and deviations. We knew there was no way of predicting who would go and who would be spared, but we couldn't help ourselves from comparing, seeking reassurance or stoking our fears. The ways we had changed were a topic of frequent conversation. There were the physical transformations, the common ones we commiserated over, hair falling out, feet too big for our shoes, vaginas which slanted differently now, like planets tilted on their axes, the *linea nigra*, which split our bellies like butcher's cuts. Then there were those idiosyncratic changes whose connections to pregnancy were tenuous and obscure. One mother was now allergic to plums and walnuts. Another had developed a gap between her front teeth. A third had noticed a silvery down sprouting in patches on her skin. It was as if, at some point as we pushed our children out, during one of those blinding flashes of pain when we briefly left our bodies, they had been swapped out for new ones, at once more intimately ours than they had ever been before, and strange to us.

These changes to our bodies inevitably yielded changes in our lovemaking. June couldn't have sex at all. The pain when her husband tried to penetrate her was excruciating; it sent her mind right back to the delivery bed at the clinic. He kept bringing her creams and ointments. He slid his fingers into her and massaged the seized muscles to try to get them to relax. He was so worried, her pain seemed so unusual. But his attempts to help her only made her more anxious. She kept expecting things to improve, for her body to settle, to acclimate, but it had been five months, which couldn't be good, could it? What if it was a sign? She said all of this in a rush, then recoiled, as if suddenly becoming aware of herself. The mothers often vacillated like this between confession and circumspection, desperate to unload their fears, yet wary that doing so might breathe life into them.

'She'll be fine. June's always been anxious,' Marie declared to me after group that day, yanking at a spent vine and coiling it on the ground at her feet. We had gone to the skinfruit grove right after group, just the two of us. This was our routine. At group we debriefed motherhood and afterward Marie and I debriefed group. I'm sure other mothers did the same, congregating here or there about town to whisper about the things we'd said and how we seemed to be doing. Sometimes Marie and I went to the grove, other times we sat on my porch or hers and worked on our baskets as our babies slept, slicing the thorns from the vines, weaving over, under, over, under, bending the spines upward to build the right shape, careful not to exert too much force and snap them. My baskets were tidy enough, but nothing compared to Marie's, the weave so tight we all joked you could fetch water in them.

'I'm sure you're right,' I said to Marie.

I plucked a fruit from a vine, its purplish black skin dusted with a powdery white residue, as if the clouds had imprinted themselves upon it. I pressed my fingers against the skin until the fruit cracked open into two hemispheres, revealing the hidden chamber within: walls of red flesh encasing white seeds, the small hollow at the center. I brought half to my mouth and pulled the flesh away from the skin with my teeth. I'd been eating the fruit for months now, ever since Iris was born, but I still couldn't describe the taste, or remember it when my mouth wasn't full of it. That was what brought us back to the grove, that negative space, not a memory of taste but the sense of a memory missing.

Other mothers had shared at group that day that configurations and maneuvers which had once sent them into rapturous spasms now produced only discomfort. We had previously loved it when our husbands sucked and even bit our nipples, but now most of the mothers expressed a complete lack of interest in this. Their breasts belonged to their babies. The sight of their husbands' mouths around their nipples revolted some, was comical to others, besides which, their nipples were sucked and chewed for hours every day, they had turned tough and senseless as the bottoms of their feet.

I didn't dare tell them that Peter still squeezed and sucked at me, sometimes drawing milk. I didn't tell them how it thrilled me to let down into his mouth instead of into Iris's, the shocking pleasure of wasted milk, spilled on sex and on Peter. I felt a bit superior, because Peter and I had found erotic potential where other couples had failed to. But then, you always had to wonder, when you were the odd one out, whether it indicated something. Why was it unimaginable to the other women that their husbands might suckle from them, while I desired it, thought of it even as I nursed Iris and was not disturbed to think of it then, with her at my breast? Did it indicate something perverse in my bond with Iris? But I loved her ferociously. I would chop anyone to bits for her. But what if that was just it? What if it was possible to love too ferociously, and to burn yourself up with it?

One day a few months after that, Liese, whose baby had terrible colic, broke down in group and confessed that once when he had been crying for hours, she squeezed him a little too hard, enough that his scrunched-shut eyes popped open in surprise. 'I never would have really hurt him,' she clarified. But she hadn't been able to keep herself from bringing him to the edge of harm, compressing the tiny body with its pliant bones and knowing she could do anything to it if she chose. She had never had a violent urge in her life and it shocked her, made her distrust herself, this new self that had spiraled out of her. 'Do you think it means something?' she whispered.

We reassured her that any mother could lose her composure under those circumstances. Besides, it had only happened the one time.

'Does that matter?' Liese said.

She was right. We had seen all our lives how the smallest moments could turn out, in retrospect, to be signs. We had seen this, but we had not understood what it would mean for us until we were mothers ourselves, when our days appeared to be made up of nothing but such minor incidents, every moment, every misstep, a possible indication.

As if on cue, Liese's baby began to cry, and she scooped him into her arms with an excessive display of tenderness. It was only natural, what Liese was doing. When a mother felt herself vulnerable she quite understandably worked to alter herself, though we didn't know whether such alterations were effective, or whether her distrust of her love, and her attempts to modify it, only singled her out all the more clearly.

'Don't overcompensate,' Marie advised succinctly.

While the rest of us reassured Liese, June stayed quiet. Marie had dismissed June's initial anxieties as typical of her, and therefore not significant. Yet the baby was seven months old now, and we couldn't help but notice how June set her down on the blanket at the start of group and then never touched her, never even really looked at her. June had always been a nervous type, but she had also been sweet, and if anything we would have pegged her as the sort to be overly attentive. This happened from time to time. The possibility of going proved too much for a mother. The peril that sent the rest of us ever more deeply into our love for our children had, for her, the opposite effect: To protect herself from it, she never bonded with her child. She surrendered her motherhood instead of waiting to find out if she would be taken from it.

When Esther announced in group that Ana was pregnant again, she would soon have 'four under four,' we didn't know what to think. Although Ana didn't attend group, she came up frequently. When a mother struggled with transitioning her baby out of a swaddle, another mother chimed in that the way Ana did it was to hold the baby's arms against his sides until he fell asleep and then slowly release them. We regularly heard things like that at group. Ana does this, Ana swears by that. She sewed matching outfits for her children. She hosted teas at her house with a dozen kinds of sandwiches and scones, vases of freshly cut jasmine and hibiscus on every surface. Her baskets were remarkable. They were not the tidiest in town, but like her violin play-ing they possessed a style all her own; she always wove a single black vine into the handles, but even if she hadn't had this signature, we could easily have picked her baskets out of a pile.

We had all been awed by the way she managed 'three under three' as if it were nothing. We admired mothers who had multiple children. The more a woman mothered, the more she revealed herself; the more risk she took on, the more deeply she felt her love for her children. When a woman stopped at one, we looked down on her somewhat, like she thought she could have it both ways, be a mother but also keep herself just a bit safer than the others. Still, to have 'four under four' was extremely rare. None of the rest of us would have dared to have so many children so quickly, before we had any sense of how things would play out.

'Doesn't it seem pretty . . . incautious?' whispered June.

'She must feel herself to be on extremely firm footing,' said Marie.

'It's *Ana*,' Esther said with exasperation. 'She'll be fine.'

I thought of Ana as only I had known her, stuffing her mouth with dirt on the mornings mothers went. What was having 'four under four' about for her? Was it simply that Ana did nothing by half measures, that if she would be a mother, she would be all mother, more than any of us? Or was it that she couldn't help herself, stop herself, from approaching the edge of what she could make herself into?

At one group, Cecily told us that lately all she wanted was some time each day to play her flute, but she couldn't get it. She didn't know why she couldn't, when babies sleep so much; the hours just slipped away. Sometimes she looked at her flute in its case and then down at her son cooing in her arms and she found herself digging her fingernails into her palms until it hurt. She felt such anger toward him in these moments, and how terrible it felt, how dangerous, to be angry at this child she loved so much. Tess said for her it was just the opposite. She could no longer summon any interest at all in watercolor, which had previously been her big passion; the Op Shop sold her botanical illustrations by the register, and they were popular birthday and anniversary gifts. 'Maybe you're just maturing out of the interest,' Marie offered. But Tess didn't think so. She thought the loss of her passion indicated not maturity but a diminishment of self. In a rare moment of earnestness, Esther chimed in that she felt the same way about her embroidery. She was known around town for the intricate stitched designs on her clothes, flowers on the back of a linen jacket, paisley on a flannel scarf. 'I haven't opened my kit in weeks,' she said. 'I hadn't even realized it until just now.' Other mothers joined in. They felt it, too, could hardly summon any interest in those things that used to give them the most pleasure, whether gardening or singing or foraging in the forest. They couldn't even really remember how it had felt to be the women who cared about these things.

Was this how it started? With these small, ordinary seeds of diminishment, which might grow until there was nothing left of you? Tess said she had instituted a system for herself. During the baby's afternoon nap, she set an egg timer for an hour and went to her easel to paint. She forced herself to do it even if she didn't feel like it that day, which most days she didn't. Sometimes the whole hour was a chore, but occasionally the old rhythms returned to her, the sweep of the wet brush over the creamy paper, the bloom of color in water when she washed the brush. Minutes would pass during which she thought of her child not at all; she forgot she was a mother and remembered what it felt like to just be Tess, painting. Some of the women said they would try similar regimens. Everyone seemed to feel better then. It always felt good to be equipped with a plan of action.

'Of course, that could be exactly the wrong approach,' Marie pointed out.

What did our affliction want from us? Did it want us to hold on to the women we had been before? Or did it want us to lose ourselves in this task, to hold nothing back from it? We could go around and around, trying to figure it out.

I felt this diminishment like the rest of us. Iris was so particular, so herself from the beginning, her hair a color that came from neither Peter nor me, the wrinkles at her knees, the way she gripped my finger with her whole hand, which I knew was a reflex but pretended was an expression of her love for me. Her body was never still, always in motion. She preferred to sleep alone in her cradle than in our arms, which according to the other mothers was unheard of. She grunted and gulped noisily when she nursed, like a queen at a feast. I didn't know most babies nursed silently until my first time at group, when the other mothers were so tickled by the voracious sounds she made. In the face of the stunning immediacy of my child, I felt my self diminish to almost nothing.

At two months, Iris was sick for the first time. She had a high fever and an unrelenting cough, worse at night, and for the better part of a week she barely slept more than a few minutes at a time. Peter wanted to share the night duties equally, but I told him one of us might as well get some rest and it ought to be him; he had patients to see during the day, teeth to pull and cavities to fill. The truth was I wanted those nights for myself. I walked the house with her for hours. Even when she finally drifted off and I laid her in her cradle beside our bed, I didn't sleep; I couldn't get enough of that vigil. I was beyond tired, exhaustion so acute I experienced it as physical pain. The days were awful, caring for her after having been awake all night; in those rare moments when sick Iris was content to be set down on a blanket, I lay on the parlor sofa and my body seemed to levitate, some aspect of myself rising out of me like steam. But what did it matter, what did I care? My child was sick, her need was total and it was mine to meet. Yet it wasn't a need for *me*, it was a need simply for a mother's hands and warmth and smell and milk. Sometimes I walked the house with her at night for so long that my arms grew numb and I could no longer feel myself carrying her. I wasn't me at all in these moments. I had disappeared, not *from* my child, but *into* her. I was only a mother. Was this dangerous, was it safe? Was it good, was it bad? I didn't know. I knew only that I loved it.

It turned out the first of us to go after I became a mother wasn't June or Liese or Tess or anyone about whom we had speculated. Iris was six months old when it came. All night a light rain had fallen, pattering on our rooftops and penetrating our dreams. When we woke we couldn't determine whether we had slept fitfully or just the opposite, with the depth one usually finds only during illness, so deep it disorients rather than refreshes. It took us some time to recognize it wasn't just the rain that had unsettled us and filled us with the sorrowful, cleansing feeling that something had been washed away in the night.

I went to the window. On the sidewalk, certain as the clouds, Sally milled about, swiveling and darting her head like a hen. She wore a ruffled lavender blouse and matching skirt, a jeweled comb in her hair.

'She out there?' Peter asked.

'What do you think?'

'Just ignore her.' He went to wash up for the day. 'Vera,' he said when he returned to our bedroom, because I was still staring out the window. He didn't understand why I couldn't shrug Sally off, and I couldn't explain why she affected me as she did, why her shamelessness, her need always to be the first one out, rooting around for the news, rankled me so.

Before we went out, while Iris was still asleep, Peter and I climbed back into bed together. Morning sex, cold and hot. My cold feet tangled with Peter's warm legs, cold hands on his soft penis, hot as a baby bird in a nest, the cold tip of his nose to my neck, warm breath rising to steam our cold morning eyes. It became our ritual. On these mornings I could not help but be reminded of the potential my body contained for dissolution. What better way to forget my body than to let myself be all body? Peter deployed different strategies than usual on these mornings. He pinned my wrists over my head, pressed me forcefully into the bed. He subjugated his pleasure to my own, as if, if only he spoiled me until there was nothing left for me to want or need, I would have no reason to go. I came two, three, four times, though the closer I got to climaxing, the more I felt myself spread and disperse, until I was no longer Vera pressed to Peter, but clouds gathering force, air sucked into the hot mouth of a sick child. Afterward, we lay together, damp and spent, and Peter touched his fingertips idly, lovingly against my cheek, playing there the cello part from the piece we had performed at our very last recital.

When we finally made our way outside, Iris wrapped to my chest, Sally homed in on us right away.

'Have you heard?' she asked, though she knew we hadn't. She'd zipped over so that she could be the one to tell us. Still, she waited for Peter and me to shake our heads before puffing herself up with an expression of great consequence and saying, 'It's Esther.'

Like I said, this was unexpected. But before I could consider it at all, Sally kept right on talking. 'Did either of you see any indications?' No doubt she hoped we might have some special insight, seeing as we had been in Esther's year and I was in group with her.

'We weren't close with her,' I said quickly, before Peter could offer the kind of polite response Sally would take for an opening.

Sally sighed; we were useless to her. 'Well.' She spread her arms to take in the scene on Hinter der Wald, neighbors streaming from their homes. 'I'd better press on,' she said, as if hers were a formally appointed role, a duty she was obligated, rather than desperate, to perform.

We made our way to the house on Gartenstrasse that had been Esther's and gathered on the lawn. The ground was soft from the night's rain. Children played together at the back of the yard, splashing in puddles and flinging mud at each other. For the first time, I joined the mothers swaying at the front, Iris warm against my chest. Our swaying seemed to hold all the truths of this moment, our horror at the loss of Esther, our relief that it had not been us, back and forth, forth and back.

Nicolas emerged from the house with baby Sarah resting peacefully in the crook of his arm. The older child, Miles, had his arms wrapped around his father's neck, clutching him. They made no sound, just stayed in this silent, shocked configuration. The wailing on this morning came from off to the side, where Esther's mother and father clung together, knees dropped in the mud. 'My baby,' her mother gasped between wails, the words inflected like it was a question, like maybe we had it wrong.

The work got underway. It was my first time going in, and I can't pretend I didn't enjoy being one of the mothers completing this task, gathering up the artifacts of Esther's girlhood, notebooks and report cards and lanyards from those days when Ana, Esther, and Lu had been so cruel to me. With Esther, the task was unusually extensive because she had been so acquisitive. There were two bureaus stuffed with clothing, an entire vanity drawer of perfumes, dozens of necklaces and earrings, and all the sundry items she had acquired over the course of her brief life: numerous purses, her racket and bicycle, her embroidery kit filled with jewel-toned threads.

As we worked we naturally discussed the indications of Esther's fate. Was she a shock? It was hard to say, because we'd never really considered her in isolation, had only ever thought of her as part of

Ana Esther Lu. Going was the first thing she did all on her own. It was Ana who had suggested to Nic that he court Esther. Ana had also suggested to Esther when to start trying for a baby, and on the whole, the shape of Esther's life had been determined much more by Ana than by herself. Esther had never given any indication of bridling at this, but, on the contrary, had always struck us as extremely contented with the arrangement. But as usual, it didn't take long before we sifted back through our recollections and found the signs. It was Marie who laid out the most flagrant clue, in her matter-of-fact way.

'We'd all noticed how clingy Miles had been with Esther recently, hadn't we?'

As soon as she said it, I couldn't believe I hadn't thought of this right away. Just the other day, in the checkout at the grocery, I had seen Miles clutching Esther's arm and kissing the length of it, working from her wrist up to her elbow, then pressing onto his tiptoes and tugging her arm down so that he could kiss her shoulder. Tess, who lived next door to Esther, had seen him stroking his mother's braid on their front porch while singing a little invented song to her, a single line he sang over and over: 'You are my sweet, sweet joy.' At the most recent children's story hour in Feldpark, several mothers now recalled that Miles, who typically liked to sit right at the front, had refused to leave his mother's lap, and had spent the hour curled into Esther at the back of the gathering, thumb in his mouth. At one point, he even tried to slip his head under her loose sweater, forcing Esther to tell him, 'We don't touch Mama there. That's private.'

How had we missed it? He had sensed his mother drawing away from him and had been trying to hold on to her. Children were so attuned to their mothers; sometimes the clearest signs occurred not in the woman but in her children, who changed as they felt her changing.

Now, revisiting her memory of Miles singing his little song to his mother, Tess recognized something else. It was Esther's reaction to her son. She had closed her eyes and seemed to bask in his affection, but when he finished singing, she hadn't hugged him or said anything to him, or in any other way reciprocated that affection. We could see it now, the selfishness that had always been there in her love for her children. Whether she realized it or not, intended it or not, she had cultivated her son's love for her own pleasure, acquired it as she acquired so many things.

We had finished our work by then, and we were gathered in the vestibule of the house. Just before we went out, June whispered, 'Do you think it hurt? Right when it happened, I mean. When her body—'

'I imagine it's quite painless,' Marie said, cutting her off. She spoke in her typical, assured way, and we nodded along, like this was a thing Marie might actually know. 'Come on, let's not dawdle,' she said, before we could think more about it. She opened the front door and we went out from the house onto the lawn.

The wheelbarrows were loaded especially high that day. Some of the young men had to make two trips just to clear it all away. It was such a big haul, such a varied and high-quality infusion of goods, that we made our way to the Op Shop immediately after the burning, which was a bit uncouth, but we all did it so there was no one to judge us. Esther's things had not yet been sorted when we arrived, and the Op Shop was turned upside down by our sifting and scavenging. I knew just what I wanted, though I doubted I would find it, what with the mess, the other women. When I came upon it almost immediately, it seemed that it had been meant for me, as if all along Esther had only stitched it, worn it, until it could be mine. The flannel scarf with the gold paisley embroidery. At the register, I declined a bag; I wrapped the scarf around my neck and wore it out of the shop into the damp afternoon.

That night in bed, Peter turned to me with a grave expression. 'I knew it would be Esther,' he said. He had done her cleaning the week before. When she opened wide and he saw her teeth, the cathedral of her palate, her black throat, there was something about it, like she was allowing him access to a secret he wasn't supposed to have.

'And you thought it meant she would go? You'd been waiting for it?'

'No, not exactly. I didn't put it together right then. But it shook me, and now I know why.'

I couldn't help but smile at his confession, which seemed more sweet than alarming: the dental occult, the mouth an augur. Still, that night when we had sex, and my mouth snapped open with pleasure, I could swear he peered inside of it, down the dark tunnel of my throat, as if the truth of me waited there.

You started to see Esther's things all over town right away. Marie in a brown turtleneck. An upper in one of Esther's old skirts. Esther's gold hoops in Di's ears. Ana strutting about town in what had been Esther's signature boots, black leather with a low heel and hook eyelets. I saw Ana everywhere in the days following Esther's going, running around town like she couldn't get enough of her own footfalls in those boots. In Feldpark, I spotted a recent upper named Corinna embroidering a kerchief with thread from Esther's old kit. Ana was there, too, pushing her youngest in his pram, looping around and around the fountain. I stayed at the park much longer than I'd intended to. I wanted to see when Ana would leave, how long it would go on. The clouds came out, everyone was heading home, but she continued her looping. I got the strange feeling we were in a competition to outlast one another, and a stranger feeling still that maybe Ana had made this happen, had cultivated Esther for going, and made of her a sacrifice, in order to keep herself.

That night when I unwrapped the flannel scarf from around my neck, I noticed a stain, a pale splotch about the size of an egg. A spit-up stain, unmistakable. An old, faded mark, faint enough that you could only see it if you were right up close. I decided I would wear it anyway.

We lived happily. In no time at all Peter and I were making arrangements for Iris's fifth birthday party. Tea at the Alpina was no longer in fashion. It would be a backyard affair with crafts and a scavenger hunt and a contest where children clasped their hands behind their backs and ate sugar doughnuts hung from our clothesline with licorice laces. We had special-ordered everything months in advance. There would be purple balloons and vases of yellow bell. For lunch, meat pies and cucumbers cut in coins, not sticks, and jelly sandwiches made triple-decker and sliced thinly to reveal their red stripes. Peter and I were merely the executors of this vision, which was Iris's from top to bottom. She had grown into a child at once dreamy and resolute, with fierce preferences about the sorts of things other children didn't even notice. By the time she was three years old she'd begun trying to choose my clothes for me in the mornings because my trousers and blouses distressed her so; she'd go into my bureau, pull out dresses or skirts, anything floral or with lace, and beg me to put them on, to wear 'pretty clothes like Sally.' Iris adored Sally and was always sneaking across Hinter der Wald to see her. She loved her pastel garments, her ruffles and her rouge and her curls. She was too young to discern the desperation in these things, or the spoilage. Sally, in turn, was so flattered by Iris's affection that she showered her with treats and gifts. Iris knew any time she popped across the street there would be some sweet or trinket waiting for her, shortbread or an old necklace of Sally's or a silk flower.

It's strange to think now that when I was pregnant with Iris, and in her early months, her particulars seemed to suggest nearly infinite possibilities for who she might become. They were clues to a temperament, but they might mean this or that, you could read them any which way. Her constant squirming, for example, could portend physical prowess, or volatility, or an aimless soul. But by then it was possible to draw a straight line from those early clues to this girl, deliberating over the best shade of purple for the balloons at her party, whether *lilac* or *lavender* or *mauve*, and hiding out beneath the kitchen table to scribble a list for the scavenger hunt: *feather, lizard, mushroom,* and, mysteriously, *wing.* Even that phrase, 'pregnant with Iris,' indicates the shift of mind I experienced, the inevitability that gathers around a child like an aura as they grow, as if, even while I carried her inside me, she was already and only could have been our Iris.

How sweet those years when Peter and I watched her reveal herself. Every day new delights, new surprises. She was such an intent child, so singular in her focus and attentions. For weeks as a toddler, she would only let us read one book to her at bedtime, over and over, no other book would do. She would gum the chosen book, suck and gnaw it until the carboard pages frayed to reveal their layers. We went through an especially intense period with a book about a rabbit family, which she called simply *Bunny*. She needed it four, five times through before she could release herself to sleep. Peter and I always tucked her in together, we never wanted to miss it, Iris in her jammies, furiously rubbing her eyes to ward off sleep, crying, 'More *Bunny*! More *Bunny*!'

Together in our bed once she was finally asleep, Peter and I said it to each other. 'More *Bunny*!' It became a code, an invitation, a statement of desire. 'More *Bunny*' and we were on one another, sucking and gnawing as Iris mouthed her beloved books, our sex giddier than it had been before Iris, fueled by our delight in her, in what we had made together and in ourselves, this family. Next thing we knew it was morning and we woke to Iris calling her deliberative order from her crib: 'Mama, come get you.'

Always, Mama. Iris was never not touching me, idly stroking me, squeezing, scratching at my skin, as if discovering her own body. While Peter tended to the teeth of the town, Iris and I spent days that seemed weeks long. For days on end when she was three years old she wanted to do nothing but stalk our backyard, staring up into the trees. 'I'm looking for the owl,' she would tell me, as if this should have been evident. When I tried to coax her inside for lunch or nap, she grew stern with me. 'Mama, you *wait*. I didn't find my owl yet.' She had learned about owls in a book of birds, one of Sally's gifts. I explained that we had no owls, they lived in places far from here, but this only sent her into a rage. '*You* don't have owls, Mama!' she shouted, and stomped her feet. I told her we should be glad we didn't have owls, they were vicious creatures. 'They steal the eggs of other birds from nests and gobble them up.' I didn't know if this was true. Regardless, she was unafraid and unconsoled. 'The eggs are baby birds,' I elaborated, but this, too, had no effect.

I told her dark things. I wanted to know the edges of her, what would make her afraid. I told her that wolves ate rabbits, that when people grew old they died and became bone. 'Okay, Mama,' she said reassuringly, as if I were seeking comfort from her in the face of these truths. I told her about the seagull, how the children shot it down and we drowned the bloody bird in the Graubach.

'Seagulls live by the sea and eagles live by the eag,' she said flatly.

I took her fishing in the Graubach. It had rained in the night, sending worms writhing up out of the ground, and we plucked them steaming from the dirt and ran them through with our slender hooks. When Iris's rod curved, she let me help her reel in her catch, then pushed me aside and crouched over the flopping fish in the grass. She stroked her hand back and forth against its scales, smooth one way, rough the other. She pressed a fingertip to its lidless eye.

Before I became a mother, I thought young children were afraid of everything. I hadn't realized there was a time before fear, when children are not afraid of the dark, or death, or beasts eating each other alive. Iris loved to poke at my torso, to press against the skin and feel it move over the ribs beneath and say, 'There's bones inside.'

Between Peter and Iris it was different. After work, he played with her while I fixed dinner. They colored and had tea parties and ran races across the yard. He delighted her with his 'jokes,' calling an apple a banana, a banana a bandanna, searching high and low for the hat on his head. They never found themselves in the convoluted tangles that were the bread and butter of our days together. If I was in the bathroom with Iris at bedtime, pleading with her to brush her teeth, Peter had only to pop his head in and say, 'Are you refusing to brush your nose?' and she laughed like it was the funniest thing she'd ever heard, then squeezed the paste onto the brush.

One afternoon, Peter and Iris were playing fairies in our yard while I wove on the porch. Suddenly Iris let out a cry and clutched her hand. At her feet, a bee limped through the wet grass. Peter tried to gather her in his arms, but she broke free of him and ran sobbing across the yard and up the porch steps to me. She climbed into my lap and I rocked her and told her soon, soon, the pain would fade. I looked across the yard at Peter. I could see the hurt in his eyes, and I wanted to wish that Iris had let him soothe her, but I couldn't make myself wish it. I wanted to wish she were not in pain, but I couldn't do that either, because the pleasure of soothing it went so deep.

I thought that I should want what Peter and Iris had, a simpler, less turbulent love, parent and child instead of the two-bodied creature Iris and I became together. But I could not make myself want it. I couldn't get enough of our push and pull, the spell we cast upon one another, our love like a secret chamber we shared, and always, no matter where we were or what we were doing, we were also there in that chamber together. I loved to love her this way, even as I worried that this love might not be what a child needs, that it might also be a kind of harm.

Peter and I stayed up half the night before Iris's party getting things ready. We sliced cucumbers, threaded licorice laces through dough-nuts, hid three glass butterflies around the yard to fulfill that mysteri-ous item on Iris's list for the scavenger hunt, *wing*. In the morning, I could still taste the bitter, talcy rubber from blowing up three dozen lilac balloons. The day was gray and breezeless, the air soft. We wor-ried it might rain but the weather held. I dabbed pink lipstick on Iris's mouth, a treat; I only did it on her birthday and supply days. She wore a purple dress she chose for its abundant sash, shiny black shoes with gold buckles, and socks with small white pearls sewn onto their ruffled cuffs. She insisted on putting on the shoes herself despite their tricky buckles, and after a long struggle she managed it. But she'd put them on the wrong feet. My stomach twisted at the sight of it, the eerie figure she made; I always felt a little panicked when she switched her shoes. But I reminded myself this was perfectly normal at her age. When I insisted she switch them, she scowled and told me they felt 'perfect and lovely' just as they were. Only when Peter intervened did she comply.

Before her guests arrived, she walked slowly around the backyard, appraising our preparations. What a little tyrant she had been in the weeks leading up to the party. Peter and I had discussed whether we were doing the right thing agreeing to her every demand, if it wouldn't be better for her to learn that a party could have cucumbers cut in lowly sticks and she could still have a good time. Now as she took in the display, her face broke into a rare, unsuppressed grin, and I squeezed Peter's hand.

We were all there, all the women with whom I'd commiserated at new mom group forever ago, our babies who were no longer babies racing across the yard in their party clothes. I loved occasions like this, so many of us gathered together, our lives showing themselves. It seemed to me this scene had always existed, like it had hung over us in the clouds until we found our way to it. Peter's brothers' children, Iris's younger cousins, smothering her in sticky hugs, which she endured with a great display of forbearance. Di's twins, eight years old now, trying hard to look unimpressed, declaring the crafts and games 'for babies' before forgetting their resistance when it was time for the doughnut contest. Marie's children looping back to ask permission each time they were offered a sweet; Marie sampling the whipped cream beside the berry salad, determining it to be too sugary, her children cheerfully eating their berries plain. Corinna, hugely pregnant, sitting with her feet propped on a chair, Nicolas fetching her water and berries and her older two, Miles and Sarah, coming over to show their crafts to their mother. Scattered across the yard, Ana's children were easy to spot, all in matching jumpers or vests; Ana herself wore a kerchief made of the same fabric, along with a dress that seemed to love her body, and her signature black boots, the soles of which she had replaced each time she wore them out. For a long time, the sight of Ana with her large brood had been so painful for me. Peter and I had always assumed we would have more children, but no more had come to us, such an unexpected blow after the ease with which I became pregnant with Iris. How inadequate I felt for years, as if my body suspected I could handle no more and so had given me no more. But by the time of Iris's party, I could imagine it no other way, and I didn't feel nearly as sensitive around Ana as I used to. It was accepted wisdom in town that a single child did not consume a mother as two or three or four did, that it left space for her, but it seemed to me the opposite was true. Iris filled my entire field of vision. I could find no want within myself for another. And I wondered if I had once been loved this fiercely.

Sally was there, too; I hadn't wanted to invite her, but Peter said we must, she lived right across the street, and besides, Iris would want her there. She wore one of her fussy outfits, a dress of brown crushed velvet with a lace collar, camera around her neck, snapping away. 'See, it's not so terrible, having her here,' Peter whispered to me as Sally took our picture, Iris rigid with happiness between us. At the party's end, Sally bestowed upon Iris a glass bottle of perfume, a special order from Mr. Phillips, a gift she was much too young for, but which she loved too dearly for me to take away.

Luckily, Peter and I had made our own special order for Iris's gift, which we presented to her after her guests had gone. A porcelain doll with real hair and hand-painted features. We were so tired after the party we did only the most cursory clean-up, plucking licorice laces from the grass, stacking leftover craft supplies next to the back door to be dealt with another time. Meanwhile, Iris cradled the doll in her arms and whispered secrets in its ear. As I watched her, I allowed myself to think that most dangerous, beloved thought: You are mine.

The next morning, Peter and I were awakened early by Iris. She stood in our doorway in her nightgown, clutching the porcelain doll by its hair so that its feet skimmed the floor. 'I feel funny,' she said. Was it her head? Her tummy? Her throat? She shook her head. 'It's not any part. Just funny.' As Peter and I surfaced from sleep we realized we felt it, too. We thought a mother must have gone, but when I went to the window, Hinter der Wald was silent and still.

'No Sally,' I said to Peter.

I took Iris downstairs to fix her breakfast. I cracked eggs into a bowl and got a bad one, brown veins in the yolk. I scooped it out and dumped it into the sink. As I ran the water, I glanced out the window. A few families had come out from their houses. They milled about uncertainly on the sidewalk.

'Stay here,' I called to Iris. I threw on my coat over my nightgown and went out. There were quite a few people about now. I approached one gathering, a newlywed couple from down the street talking with an elderly widower.

'What's happening?' I asked.

The young bride furrowed her brow, as if trying to do a big sum in her head. 'We think it's Sally,' she said. 'We think it's Sally who's gone.'

At first, we were very confused. Sally was decades older than the women who usually went, and she was not a mother. It took some time before we believed it was her at all. Initially, we thought she must be sick in bed, which would explain her absence. Then Peter and a few of the other men on Hinter der Wald went into her house and confirmed she wasn't there, and confirmed, too, that everything in her house was consistent with going. Her purse rested on the table in the front hall. All the shoes we could ever recall Sally wearing were in the rack in her closet: the blush pumps, the old-fashioned ankle boots with the satin laces. Her quilt was rumpled but not tossed back, suggesting she'd slept beneath it and had not left it. Still, we thought it must be some elaborate stunt. Sally must have arranged things as if she'd gone and then retreated to a spot above town to see the morning unfold. 'Probably watching us as we speak,' people kept saying. She'd always needed to be at the center of things, always weaseled her way in, and it was easy enough to see a stunt like this as the culmination of such behavior.

But by late morning Sally still hadn't turned up, and we began to accept that she really had gone. As I said, this baffled us, and that morning theories about what her going meant spread at a furious pace. Perhaps it had been a coincidence all this time that only mothers went. Maybe the first few women, long ago, had been mothers, so we thought it was only ever mothers, so we nearly all became mothers, desperate to reveal ourselves to ourselves. Others saw Sally's going as a sign that our affliction was spreading. Perhaps soon other childless women would go, and who next? Husbands? Children? Would our affliction spread until it came for us all? It really was a shame this hadn't just been some ridiculous stunt of Sally's, because she would have loved to see the stir she was causing.

But as with any woman's going, soon a more plausible explanation emerged. It was a nurse, a white-haired woman, long since retired, who told us that Sally wasn't childless. She had been a mother, very briefly. The baby had been born too soon. Sally had barely started to show when it happened and she hadn't yet made news of her pregnancy public. 'Sally was very discreet back then,' the nurse said. She'd had several miscarriages and this had made her cautious. Some of the older people in town confirmed this portrait of Sally once the nurse laid it out. Come to think of it, we did recall a time when Sally was a different sort of person, not the frivolous woman we loved to scorn because she made it so easy. Those of us old enough to remember this shift in Sally's temperament had always attributed it to the death of her husband, a foolish death, diving drunkenly into the Graubach where it was shallow; as if, having debased herself by marrying him, she felt compelled to continue debasing herself with her behavior in his absence. But now that we thought about it, it was really only in the last year of his life that anybody could recall her husband's drinking being a problem. We remembered him as a drunkard because that was how he died. According to the nurse, who was our only source on the matter, the doctor who delivered the baby having died years ago, Sally's child lived only a few hours. She never breathed outdoor air. She never cried, didn't make a sound, could not see or suckle. She could only be held, and rocked, and she was, and that was her life; two hours, maybe three, the nurse could not recall exactly, during which Sally and her husband cradled her and sang to her in whispers, the whole small family squeezed together in the clinic bed, Sally still bloody and the floor still streaked with her blood from the delivery. 'Clean it later,' Sally had told the nurse, and ordered her away.

All this time we'd misunderstood Sally, and she had let us. We had attributed her behavior to her childlessness when the truth was just the opposite. Sally was as she was because she had been a mother, because she was one; you could not travel back across the threshold of motherhood once it had been breached. She was a mother but she was without her child. She had no needs to meet, no place to put her love, and we thought this might explain why she had lingered so long, why our affliction had come for her at such an advanced age, and we wondered whether she had welcomed it.

I saw Sally barging into our house five years earlier, just after Peter and I returned from the clinic with Iris, with her fricassee and her camera, Sally being Sally, nosing in, trying to render herself indispensable. No, I saw now. She let us think this of her, let us think whatever we wanted. I saw her lifting Iris from my arms, closing her eyes and rocking her and breathing in her newborn smell. That was what she was really after, that moment, a warm bundle in her arms who might be any baby, might be hers, a version of her child who had what she needed to live. What was it she had said to me? 'Nobody can ever take this from you.'

We assembled on Sally's front lawn, but we weren't waiting for anyone to emerge from the house, so our standing around felt rather purposeless. Eventually Peter and I took the lead. Sally was our neighbor, after all, and it was only now that it really occurred to us she had no living family and no real friends, that we were likely the closest people she'd had. How quiet it was as we completed the usual tasks, with no husband or children or parents to wail for her, or to put forth any resistance to our work. Off went Sally's things, her lacy blouses and ruffled skirts, her jeweled clips and combs, her floral dresses and her nightgowns with the smocked bodices and the pintucked hems. Unsurprisingly, there was not the usual rush to the Op Shop, Sally's style having been so particular, and at first we all said what a useless haul it was. But women did trickle in, and most left with something.

In the weeks that followed you'd see women with some frill or sparkle and think how these items softened and brightened things.

When it came to piling up Sally's image, we ran into complications. For all the photographs Sally had taken of us, it turned out she hadn't taken any of herself. She must have had wedding portraits, but we didn't find them. Maybe she had disposed of them herself after her husband died. In the end we found only a single photograph, tucked in the drawer of her nightstand: Sally and her husband and the little child cocooned together in the clinic bed, Sally and her husband's faces turned down to the tiny babe, a flash of reddish forehead beneath a yellow cap. Peter set this one photograph on the ground, lit a match, and held it to the edge until it caught. It was such a light, flimsy thing. As it burned it was borne aloft on the breeze, like a bird aflame, flapping in the air until it was ash.

It must have been a week later that Peter and I finally got around to putting away everything from Iris's party, leftover paper and paints and glitter and glue. I found the three glass butterflies amid the mess and ran them up to Iris's room, set them atop her dresser with her other precious things, her ballerina music box and her kaleidoscope and the old-fashioned hand mirror in which she liked to admire herself. When I got downstairs, Peter was sitting at the kitchen table.

'What are those?' I asked.

'Photos from Iris's party. Found them with everything.' He shrugged and continued flipping through them. 'Too bad,' he said. 'You must have moved.' He set the stack down and got up to put away the rest of the craft supplies.

I took the pile in my hands. The picture on top was the family portrait we had taken in front of the yellow hibiscus. Iris had worked her face into the romantic gaze she loved to affect, her hands tucked behind her, puffing out her dress. Peter grinned, one hand on top of Iris's head, the other around my waist. The yellow blossoms, Peter, Iris, all of it was sharp and clear. Only my image was blurred. A transparent double drew away from the primary form, as if, at the moment the photograph was taken, I had darted away. Peter's hand around my waist seemed to grasp an apparition. I remembered posing for the photograph, standing with Peter and Iris, the feeling of his hand around my waist. I was certain that when it was taken, I hadn't moved. I had been standing perfectly still.

I told myself not to panic. It was a children's legend, a scary story. I kept busy. I cooked elaborate dinners: beef in pastry, potatoes sliced wafer thin and baked in cream. I cut dahlias from our garden and arranged them around our house in vases. I threw myself into Iris. We made clay beads, berry ice pops, papier-mâché lanterns. I got together with Marie for tea. I didn't mention the photograph. Marie hadn't put stock in the legend even when we were girls. I said nothing to Peter, either, because it really was a girls' thing, that story. It had been clear when he saw the photograph that it didn't signify anything to him, and surely that was right: It was nothing, a chance occurrence, most likely caused by the unsteady hand of the woman who had taken the photograph.

But a few nights after I saw the picture, I was in the kitchen slicing turnips when suddenly my hand that held the knife wouldn't move. I stared at it, willed it, but I couldn't make it go, lift, slice. My hand seemed to have separated itself from my mind's control. Iris was at the kitchen table, standing on a chair and 'cooking' by mixing sugar with white cheese and dried beans. I could hear the gentle streaming as she tipped a spoonful of sugar into the bowl. 'Would you care to try my ice cream, Mama?' she asked, and just like that it passed: I jerked, my hand moved, and before I went over to 'taste' her creation, I sliced the rest of the turnips and tossed them in the pot for supper.

At Feldpark a few days later, it was my mouth that separated itself from my control. The fountain had been drained for its annual cleaning. Iris sat in the dry basin with Mags and Rufina, her threesome, cozied together and whispering. Ana sat on the bench next to mine. One of her sons was climbing the crying woman, shoes pressing on her bare feet, hands gripping her neck to gain purchase and hoist himself up. I turned away for a moment, and when I looked back, Iris wasn't with Mags and Rufi; she had begun to walk along the fountain's curled lip, arms stretched to either side, a fall of several feet onto stone if she lost her balance. I tried to call to her *Get down! Get down!*, but my mouth defied me. I thought the words over and over, but they wouldn't come. Finally I heard them, 'Get down!,' only it wasn't my voice that said them, it was Ana's. Iris hopped down at once. I blinked and everything was as it always was, and I was obliged to turn to Ana and say, 'Thank you,' and my mouth cooperated without any trouble.

'Such a daring girl.' Ana said it like she was praising Iris, but I understood she was also judging me for not attending to my child's safety. When I didn't respond, she squinted at me. 'Are you feeling all right, Vera?'

'Why wouldn't I be?'

Ana shrugged. 'No reason.'

I called to Iris and told her it was time to go. She started to protest, which was typical of her; it was always impossible to get her to leave her friends. But then she looked at me, and something she saw stopped her. She said a quick goodbye to Mags and Rufi and followed after me.

I began to notice other changes in Iris. She started to hold her bowels for days, determined not to let them out. She had never done this before. When she could hold them no longer, she pulled me into the bathroom with her like a much younger child. I sat on a wooden footstool beside the toilet and Iris clasped my hands and yelped in pain as she pushed out movements hard and gray as river stones. She began waking at night. I would fetch her a glass of water, rub her back, sing to her, but she begged me to stay, which was also unlike her; she had always required her own space and slept soundly in it. I took to sliding under her quilt with her. As soon as I was beside her she drifted quickly back to sleep. I lay awake. I pressed myself to her small, hot body, breathed in her hair, her night breath, unpleasant yet precious because it was hers. I stared at a small brown scab on her arm until it seemed as miraculous as a star.

Our affliction had come for mothers since the beginning, and now I feared it was coming for me. To stop it from happening I would do anything, become anyone. But I didn't know what to do or who to become. Even if I did know, would it matter? Was there anything I could do to counteract myself, to give my child something other than that which I possessed? When she threw one of her fits because I forbade her to pull the petals from the flowers in the garden at Feldpark for *loves me, loves me not,* and I held her writhing body against mine so tightly I couldn't say whether I wished to calm her or consume her, was that the tangled, mysterious love known to all mothers and their children? When she sat on the toilet and each time she bore down, I, too, held my breath and clenched my body, was that simply a mother's bond with her child, or was it something else? How much of my love was a love for Iris, and how much was a love for the way she unburdened me of myself, and was this unburdening what I sought above all in loving her? Was it the spoiled root of my love?

I thought of those nights when Iris was an infant and I walked the floors with her until the ground beneath my feet seemed to tilt and the heaviness of her small body in my arms turned me weightless, and I seemed not to be Vera at all, and how I loved it, loved it. Maybe my going had already begun then. Maybe it had never not been in me, growing all this time while I thought I got everything I ever wanted.

I tried to tell Peter. My image in the photograph, transparent and blurred. My hand and mouth separating from my control. He reasoned it was most likely the photograph itself setting off these incidents. It had terrified me, and my mind had spun out these psychic flickerings, these strange physical phenomena in response.

I mentioned the changes in Iris. Peter admitted he had noticed them, too.

'The fiendish fives,' he said.

I shook my head. 'She senses it.'

'Vera, it's a phase. And you know the things about phases.'

'They pass.' It was a thing we said whenever Iris tried our patience.

We had sex then. I pricked him more deeply than usual, drawing more blood. But even with his blood on my tongue, I couldn't lose myself in the act. I was too distracted. I had to think of wolves chasing me down and tearing at my flesh to finish.

How could I distinguish a sign from my mind playing out its fear of signs? What was the difference between how it felt to go and how it felt to be consumed by a fear of going?

We lay together quietly a long time. I wanted to fall into Peter's certainty, and to leave it alone, but I couldn't help myself. 'Isn't it possible you're wrong?' I asked, when he was nearly asleep.

He lifted his head off the pillow. 'I suppose so.'

'And then?' I wanted him to say that he would seal shut our house so the clouds could not reach me, that he would pierce my skin and drink from me until our affliction could not determine which of us it wanted.

He was silent a moment, considering. 'Then we will wail for you.'

The next afternoon, when Peter was at work and Iris was playing at Rufina's and I would not be missed, I went to the forest. I carried my basket as if I were going to gather skinfruit, but when I reached the grove I kept walking, up into the mountains. I climbed past where the trees changed from the sort whose leaves turned white and fell to evergreen varieties and finally to the spindly mangled specimens that grew on the highest reaches of the mountain, where the Graubach was nothing but a trickling of water over rock. The higher I climbed, the more a terror came over me that Peter and Iris were not real and never had been. When I descended the mountain I would find the town gone, in its place only more wilderness, trees choking in sweet flowering vines, goats moving in packs where I could have sworn Hauptstrasse had been just that morning. The goats would snort and stamp at the earth right where Rapid Ready had once been, and where there was now only a dense thicket of thorns. If I found an opening in the thicket and pressed my eye to it, I would see on the other side of it a room with empty shelves in which a girl stood, hair falling out of her braids, holding a silver frame with a picture of a family inside, mother, father, daughter, and I would know that the girl was me and that I, grown Vera with my husband and child, was nothing but a fantasy conjured by her wanting mind.

I had stayed too long in the mountains. The clouds were gathering, cold in my mouth and heavy in my braid. I'm not sure what compelled me to stretch my hand out in front of me. Maybe I knew already what I would see, or wouldn't; maybe this was what had drawn me into the mountains to begin with: my fingertips gone, vanished into the clouds. I could see the silhouettes of trees in the distance, but I could not see the edges of myself, inches away.

I began to play a game. The next morning, I found myself stepping into the Op Shop. From the bargain bin, I lifted a pair of brown loafers and a blue linen dress. When no one was looking, I slipped them into my basket. At home, I stuffed them in the chimney.

Suppose I did not allow it to happen? Suppose I fled instead? I could leave all of my possessions behind, bring with me only these stolen items, and in the morning when they woke, they would not know I had done something other than vanish. *You could leave this place.* The stranger Ruth had said this to me. Of course, I wouldn't really do it; this game, the thefts and the chimney, it was just a way to relieve the terrible pressure of these days. After all, Ruth's suggestion was the kind only a person from elsewhere could make, a woman who did not understand us or the bargain we had made. Leave and go where? There was only here, only us. Besides, what mother would not cling to her child until she no longer had hands with which to cling? Until she was nothing, air?

· · ·

The more I lost purchase on myself, the more vivid Iris became. I couldn't tear my eyes away from her. Iris collecting stones in our yard and arranging them on the porch rail. Iris letting out her braids at night, brushing her hair while humming some secret tune. Iris getting a berry seed stuck between her teeth at breakfast, opening her mouth wide to me so that I could dislodge the seed with my fingernail. Every moment was doubled, both itself and the approaching loss of such moments. Every joy delivered the most exquisite pain.

I tried to console myself that this was the worst of it, this terrible waiting, when I was still with my child but knew it would not last, that soon there would come a final moment, an end. Once our affliction came for me, I wouldn't have to feel the loss of her. I would simply be gone. I might not even know it when it came. Perhaps my mind would vanish right in time with my body and my going would be achieved without my own awareness of it.

For Iris, too, the pain would be brief. She would wail, she would rage, but it would pass. Soon, Peter might have a new wife, and Iris a new mother, and they might love her. There would be nobody left then who knew that there had been a mother named Vera who slid her fingernail between her daughter's teeth and prized loose a small white seed. Iris and me and everything we were to one another: this, too, would simply be gone.

I went back into the mountains. Again I knew I should descend before the clouds came, and again I stayed. This time when I stretched out my arm into the clouds, my entire hand vanished.

Back down below, when I reached the edge where the forest met our yard, something pale and bright caught my eye against the black earth. It was Iris's doll, limbs smeared and hair caked with dirt, eyes open to the clouds.

Iris awoke in the middle of the night calling, 'Mama! Mama!'

I went to her, bare feet on the floor. She lay curled beneath her quilt, hair damp against her pillow. I slipped under the quilt beside her, swept the wet locks away from her neck. The skin there was soft and fleshy; I could still see the baby she had once been. Her body gave off heat that seemed made of her innocence, of everything that had not yet happened to her, all the truths she did not yet have to know.

'Mama! Mama!'

'I'm right here, Iris,' I said, and kissed her damp neck. 'Would you like a glass of water?'

'Mama! Mama!'

'Iris, it's me. I'm here. Mama is here.'

'Mama! Mama!'

Was she dreaming? But her eyes were open. She was staring right through me, as if I weren't there at all.

The next morning, I stopped in at the lingerie shop. They had the prettiest bra in stock, cream with a rosette between the cups. I waited until the counter girl was busy with another customer to remove it from its hanger and tuck it in the bottom of my basket. When I returned home, I hid it with the dress and the loafers in the chimney.

I decided to fix a goat stew for dinner. I watched the butcher chop the meat with his cleaver, wiping the watery pink traces of blood on his apron. The grocery had star anise in stock, a rarity, and I tossed the stars into the hot oil in the pot and watched them clatter. When Peter came home he inhaled the aroma deeply and hugged me from behind as I stirred the red broth. But the stew was nothing but bones, bits of them studding the meat like teeth. I could make no sense of these bones, of where they had come from on the beast, what parts of her we ate.

I walked into the mountains every afternoon now. I couldn't keep myself away, even as I suspected it might be the very act of monitoring my vanishing that propelled it. One day my wrist vanished into the clouds. The next, I held the end of my braid, stretched it away from me as far as it would go, and its narrow tip dissolved into the air.

Back in town, I drifted in and out of the shops. I selected a pair of silver candlesticks from a display at the Op Shop. At the jewelry store, a strand of pearls and a garnet ring. I waited until the shopkeepers were busy before concealing these items in my basket. At home, I added them to my collection.

One afternoon up in the mountains, the clouds came and when I looked down I could no longer see my feet anchoring me to the ground. My body seemed to levitate above the earth. I ran then, on feet I could not see. I was nearly down the mountain, dashing through the grove, when I heard a voice call my name. The clouds were thick now; nobody should have been out. Yet there, beneath a tangle of vines, stood Ana. I stopped at once.

'Just here for some fruit,' I said, raising my arm to display the basket that dangled from its crook.

'Putting up preserves,' she said, gesturing down at her own basket.

Lies, both, and we knew it. We should be home now. Had she seen me going into the mountains, noted my daily ascents, and positioned herself here, lying in wait for me? She wore her black boots, and she pressed up onto her tiptoes, reached her long arm into the vines and pulled at a fruit until it broke free.

Beneath the vines the ground was littered with fallen, trampled fruits spilling their red insides.

'Finding enough?' I asked.

'Plenty.'

I watched as she plucked several more fruits from the vines.

She squinted at me. 'Are you sure you've been feeling all right?'

'Very well, Ana. And you?'

'Right as rain.'

Her basket was full now. 'I should be getting back to my family,' she said. 'So should you, don't you think?'

Before she left, she bent down and picked up one of the fallen fruits from the ground, split and oozing and covered in dirt. She brought it to her mouth and bit, skin and all. 'Sleep well tonight, Vera.'

On my way home, I stopped at the leather goods shop. I walked its aisles, breathing in the scent of cured skins. The proprietor was an old man, and he made all of the goods in the shop himself. He knew how to turn a goat's hide into the supplest kidskin, and to sew it into a pair of shoes, a wallet, a briefcase. He was a gifted craftsman, we all said so, but he carried the scent of his work on him, as if his own skin were cured leather, tainted with the memory of blood. No woman had married him and he had no children, and no young people had expressed interest in learning this trade from him. When he died our town would no longer have a leather goods man, and this shop would become something else, and if you wanted a leather piece you would have to place a special order with Mr. Phillips. The proprietor was dozing now, in his chair behind the counter. He didn't see me take a small satchel down from a hook and hide it beneath the gingham cloth in my basket, where there should have been fruit.

That night, I did for my family the things I had always done for them. I cooked supper, pork and cabbage over rice. I used red cabbage to entice Iris, but this backfired; the cabbage stained the meat with garish violet blotches.

Iris pushed her plate away. 'I want something else.'

'Your mother worked hard to cook this meal,' Peter said.

'I still don't like it.'

'You haven't tasted it.'

'I still *won't* like it.'

I listened to Peter say all the things to Iris I knew he would say. He told her that someone had worked hard to raise this animal, had woken at dawn and gone out to mix slop for its breakfast. The piggy, too, had worked hard, growing big and strong just for her, so that she could eat him for her supper. Patient Peter, who saw in all things the patient labor of others, and wished for his daughter to see this, too. I think it hurt him more than it hurt me when she rejected the dinners I cooked. He was always trying to protect me, even from Iris. He didn't understand that a mother and daughter cannot be protected from one another, that the harms that pass between them cannot be mitigated because they are also expressions of love.

'I want a deal,' she said.

'Iris,' Peter began, but I put my hand over his on the table. I reached my spoon across to Iris's plate and moved two chunks of pork, a few strands of cabbage, and a spoonful of rice to one side. 'Eat that and I'll make you jelly bread.'

Always, this bargaining. If you eat this, I'll make you that. If you put on your shoes right this minute, you can bring dolly. If, then. This for that.

Iris stabbed at a chunk of meat and brought it slowly to her mouth with a grimace. She parted her lips and pulled the meat from the tines of the fork with the backs of her teeth. 'Yuck.'

But I could tell from the way she chewed, molars sinking deeply into the meat, tongue pressed against it to release its juice, that she loved it. With these nightly ordeals she deprived herself of food she wanted in order to reject what I had made for her, and my love for her, and in so doing to test its limits. She survived on suppers of jelly bread, sugar when she craved spice, and each night I labored over roasts and stews she rejected on sight, but I did not stop making this food, I loved her and loved her.

This child would grow, and I would not get to see it. She would cry and I would not be there to soothe her. She would play music I could not hear. She would learn a thousand new things and I would have taught her none of them. She would marry and become a mother, and I would not be there to teach her, and one day, if she climbed into the mountains and looked down and found that her feet had vanished beneath her, I would not be there to hold her, keep her. And if she went, I would not be there to wail for her.

After we put Iris to bed, Peter and I made love. If he sensed the change in me, if he knew what was coming, he gave no indication of it. When I slipped the pin from my braid and pricked his skin and tasted his blood, I hoped that this matter of him inside me might be enough to pull me back from the edge, even as I knew it would not. Within minutes he was fast asleep, and I lay beside him, taking in the gentle details of his slumber: the way he cleared his throat in his sleep, the tensionless set of his brow, his curls shining in the moonlight. When Iris called out for me, I lowered my face to his and kissed him. Then I went to her.

I slid into the narrow bed and nestled my body against hers, so small and so warm. Her elbow jabbed my chest. Her behind pressed against my stomach. I felt a puff of air against my belly. She had farted, and a moment later I caught the smell that was only hers. I pressed myself up against her.

It began to happen then. I could not feel Iris against me. I could see that my body touched hers, but I couldn't feel her, or the heaviness of the quilt over me, the weight of my body against the bed, the cloud-cool air against my skin. It would be here soon now, so very soon: the edge, the end, that last moment before my self and my love for my child vanished from this earth. I had only to lie here until it came, as mothers had done since our affliction began. How badly I wanted to do this, to hold Iris until I was nothing, and never have to know a life without her. Then someday, years from now, someone might come upon the items I had stowed in the chimney. It might be Peter, or Iris, or Iris's new mother, or a brother or sister that mother had been able to give her. And they wouldn't know what to make of these odd, dusty things, which would be just one more mystery in this place of mysteries.

The clouds thickened around me, white upon white, and some part of me began to rise out of myself to join them, and I felt nothing, nothing, but a terrifying weightlessness. Soon there would be no choice.

My eyes filled with tears, and when they rolled down my cheeks they produced no sensation whatsoever, and when they landed in Iris's hair, and I pressed my tongue to them, I tasted nothing. And I could not do it. I could not make myself stay, could not let myself go, while I still had feet on which to flee. If the only way to go on loving my child was to run from her, then I would run.

I pressed my face against the back of Iris's neck. I whispered into her perfect ear: 'I love you. You are mine. Remember me.' Useless, I knew.

I still hoped my words might wake her. *I love you, too, Mama,* she might say, in her sweet, half-asleep voice, and I would not be able to pull myself away. But she did not wake. I lifted the quilt away from myself and slid out of her bed. In the doorway, I paused and looked back at her, and tried to burn the image of my sleeping child into my memory.

To the chimney. I had not allowed myself to believe when I stole these items, when I hid them, that I would make use of them. I stripped down right there, naked in our parlor. I slipped into the bra, the dress, the loafers. I rolled up my nightgown and stuffed it into the satchel along with the candlesticks, the pearls, the garnet ring. I went to the closet in the hall and took down the box from my father's house and removed from it the only thing I had that nobody else had ever seen, the one keepsake I could take with me because no one would miss it when they came to burn my image and remove my possessions from our house, which would by then, by morning, no longer be mine. The photograph from the stranger Ruth. I put this in the satchel. From my purse on the table by the front door I removed as many coins as I dared. Then I opened the door and went out onto the lightless street.

Past our neighbors' houses on Hinter der Wald. Past the Alpina and Feldpark, the crying woman's tears lost in the thick night clouds. Onto the supply road, its steep pitch difficult to manage in my new loafers, which were ill-fitting and chafed at my heels. Because of the steepness of the slope, in no time, when I turned and glanced back the way I had come, the town had slipped from view.

III

descended the supply road until it met the train tracks, and then I followed the tracks. I stumbled through the darkness, tripping on roots and rocks and letting vines snatch at my ankles, branches whip my face, frantic and tumbling as in the final moments of a terrible dream.

I walked for hours, and when the sky lightened I found myself in an unfamiliar world. These were the lowlands with their steaming thickets, heat that pressed itself into my mouth and down my throat. I stopped to empty leaves and stones from my loafers. The shoes had chafed my heels bloody. At my feet, I saw a rubble of small black pellets, tapered at one end and teeming with white worms. They seemed to demand my attention, though it wasn't until I slid my raw feet back into the loafers and continued on that I put together why, that I had never seen dung this exact shape, which must have come from a creature unknown to me.

Peter and Iris would be waking now and finding me gone. I had been so careful. I had taken with me nothing they would miss, left everything just as it would have been if I had submitted to our affliction, giving them no cause to suspect what I had done instead. Was Iris wailing for me? Was Peter holding her? I placed my arms across my chest and swayed as if I held Iris, a baby, as if it might be possible to sooth her from where I stood in the jungle, running from her.

I traveled for so long with no end in sight that I began to wonder if this really was a kind of dream. Maybe I hadn't fled at all, but had vanished into the clouds like all the other mothers, and this was the purgatory where gone mothers went, following tracks that stretched through the jungle for all eternity. But abruptly the thickets parted and I found myself at the edge of a clearing, at the center of which stood a small stone building with black shutters. One of the windows was halfway open, and on the other side of it a man was seated before a cash register. Outside of the building, a few yards from the tracks, was a green bench. This must be the train station. I straightened myself up as best I could, brushing burs from the hem of my dress, smoothing my hair, and walked to the window and asked the price of a ticket to the nearest city. The man had pocked cheeks and a beard strewn with crumbs. If he wondered who I was or where I had come from or what I planned to do in the city, he didn't show it. He stated the fare. I had just enough coins, and I retrieved them from my satchel and passed them through the window, careful not to let our fingertips touch. 'Be an hour 'til it comes,' he said. He passed my ticket through the window without so much as looking at me.

I sat on the bench and waited. I was certain an hour must have passed and the train still hadn't arrived. It was full daylight by then and the bench had no shade. I had never experienced sunlight like this, unfiltered by clouds, and it seemed to beat down upon me. We would be gathering now on our lawn. The young mothers swaying. Di and Marie crying for me. The others chattering among themselves about the indications they had seen. Would they focus on Iris's party, how I had catered to her every wish, and would they decide that there was something unusual about my deference to my child, as if I trusted her more than myself? Would they comb all the way back to the new mom group, how hesitantly I had burped newborn Iris, and conclude that I had always lacked a certain instinct for the tasks of motherhood? And would they be wrong? What greater evidence could there be than me, here on this bench?

I had by then been waiting much longer than an hour. A few times I glanced back at the man behind the window, and when we made eye contact he shrugged disinterestedly, as if he didn't know what I had expected. I must have waited half a day when at last the train came roaring down the track, breaks squealing and swallowing me up in clouds of brown dust. When it came to a stop, a door opened and a man in a navy uniform hopped down onto the gravel beside the track and set a small stepstool there. I offered him my ticket, he barely looked at it, and I climbed onto the train.

It wasn't crowded. To my great relief I found an empty compartment and sat by the window, which was filthy, smudged on the interior and streaked on the exterior with grime in thin slanted columns. They would be burning my image now, smoke rising to meet the clouds. Near the bottom of the glass I saw the greasy handprint of a child. I pressed my hand over it and closed my eyes.

The train pulled away from the station slowly, but in no time it gathered speed, and soon I was traveling through space more quickly than I ever had before. For a long time, we continued through jungle, which pressed so near to the window that I grew nauseated, a feeling not helped by the air inside the car, which was hot and still and stank of fuel and coffee. Every hour or so we reached a small station identical to the one where I had boarded, stone with black shutters, a green bench, beyond it a crude settlement. A few hours into my journey, we left the jungle for land that must once have been jungle but was no longer. The sunlight streamed in powerfully, strobing through the scant trees along the tracks, and the interior of the train grew hotter still. My dress stuck to my back with sweat and my thighs chafed against the upholstered seat, which released the odors of other bodies into the heat. It became difficult to breathe. There were large towns now, stations with raised platforms and brick buildings several stories tall. But this was only a small portion of what we passed. Mostly, the land was neither settlement nor wilderness but something in between, mile after flickering mile of fields overtaken by bramble and brier, squat buildings stripped of their paint and suffocating in creepers. I kept my face steadfastly to the window, trying to absorb the scale of it, how much forsaken space there was out here, places it seemed nobody would miss if you snipped them from the face of the world. I wondered what had become of the people who once cultivated these fields and labored in these buildings, and what would become of me, in this world into which I was heading.

I was so fixated on the view that I gave quite a jump when the door to my compartment opened. A man stood there, white-haired, clutching a wooden cane.

'Do you mind?' he said, and continued to stand in the doorway.

Were the compartments assigned? Was this his? 'I'm sorry,' I said. 'I didn't realize.' I gathered up my satchel, face hot.

'Do you mind if I join you,' he said, looking at me curiously.

I was too flustered to reply. I nodded, sat back and gestured at the empty seat across from me. He lowered himself slowly onto it and leaned the cane beside him. The handle was a silver fish, its lips opened wide to consume the polished shaft. I was uncertain what to do now, what was expected. I smiled, trying to show I was friendly without being too forward, then turned back to the window. We were nearer to the city now. We stopped every twenty minutes or so, and the platforms were crowded, and at each stop I could feel the human presence on the train swell.

'You heading to the city?' the man asked.

I nodded.

'Me, too,' he said, and I understood I should have asked him this. 'To visit my grandchildren.'

'I'm on holiday,' I said.

'Off to see the cathedral?'

I told him I was, though I hadn't known there was a cathedral in this city.

'Go early.'

I thanked him for the advice and told him I would. He asked where I was visiting from, and I gave the name of a town we had passed several hours after I boarded. He seemed to appraise my dress, my loafers, and he shrugged.

'Husband didn't want to see the cathedral?'

I rubbed my index finger against my wedding band. At home it was always slightly cool to the touch, but here it was warm.

'Just taking a little time to myself,' I said as casually as I could manage.

'Children.' I only understood it was a question when he paused and waited for my response.

'Three boys.' I knew I had to lie, that I could not be myself here. As if, if I said I had one child, a daughter named Iris, this man would know I had left her, and would go out into the corridor and shout and rap his cane and the people on the train would rip me from this compartment and toss me onto the tracks and say in many voices, 'Go back. We do not want you here.'

It turned out this man was the youngest of three boys. His mother and his brothers were dead now. His grandchildren were teenagers and they had no time for him. They never wrote to him except to ask for money, which he gave them, and yet here he was, traveling a long way to see them. I didn't know the first thing about how to respond to such a terrible story; I had no experience with them.

'It's their mother's fault,' he said, his tone shifting sharply. 'She could never handle them. I kicked her out when she was seventeen and she ended up here.' He gestured out the greasy window, for the train was slowing, and outside I saw a vast network of tracks and signals and beyond them buildings as far as the eye could see. He spoke as if these things he had done and that had been done to him, his rejection of his daughter and her children's rejection of him, did not quite connect, one to the next. The train had not yet stopped, but outside our compartment people lined up in the corridor, pressing and jostling each other. The man gripped the fish on the handle of his cane and stood. 'If you ask me, the cathedral is a disappointment. You should have taken your holiday someplace else.'

This station was not like the ones the train had passed on my journey to the city. There must have been at least twenty platforms, all of them feeding into a central hall with a domed ceiling made entirely of glass. The hall was more massive than I had ever imagined an interior space could be, as if you had enclosed all of Feldpark, and it would have been magnificent had the glass dome not been allowed to turn filthy, filmed with grime and spackled with bird droppings. It was the end of the day and the hall was crowded, so much so that when I climbed to the top of a curving staircase to take in the scene, I could scarcely see the floor, the whole thing seemed to be made of a seething mass of bodies hurrying this way and that and producing a deafening clamor. I kept trying to pick someone out and watch them, a tall woman in a drab brown sweater, a man in a gabardine coat, but I lost each of them

within moments to the tumult of human movement, all this purposeless urgency, above which birds like the bird in the stranger Ruth's
photograph, soot-gray with iridescent throats, swooped and dove,
trapped within the glass dome.

By the time I found my way out onto the street it was nearly dark.
Every face was a stranger's face, and I let them flow through me. I
needed information, directions, but over and over I lost the courage to
stop someone and ask them. A few times I did call out, 'Excuse me,'
but the strangers brushed past me as if my voice didn't register at all.
Finally, I saw a mother with a small child coming up the sidewalk, and
I felt relieved; a mother would help, a mother would show her child
what helping looked like. Sure enough when I called to her, she did
stop.

'I'm sorry to bother you,' I said. 'Can you tell me where I might
find the Op Shop?'

'The what?'

'I have things I need to sell.'

She raised her eyebrows, tightened her grip on her child's hand.
'You won't find that sort of thing around here. Try by the canals.'

I felt the little boy's eyes on me, dark and wet. He seemed to know
that I was a mother and that my child was not with me, that I had
left her. Before I could ask where I might find the canals, the mother
tugged the little boy's hand and they hurried past me.

The train station was right in the city center, and after walking
another few blocks in no particular direction I came upon a map with
an alphabetized list of the city's districts beneath it, one of which was
Canal End. It was off to the east, and I walked through the night toward it. As I walked, the spire of the cathedral passed in and out of
view, appearing sometimes to be drawing nearer, other times farther

away, the way the moon follows you in the sky, until at last it slipped from view for the final time. I continued down a thoroughfare that, according to the map, would lead me eventually to Canal End. For several blocks, every shop sold porcelain goods, pitchers and vases and urns; next it was flowers, then hats, then two blocks of shops that sold nothing but iron bric-a-brac, each store so cluttered with objects they spilled onto the sidewalk. When I reached the canal I stood on the edge, hands against the corroded iron railing. The water was black and stagnant; there was no current here, only the sloshing against the canal walls, like water in a bath. According to the map this, too, was the Graubach; it stalled here before traveling a thousand miles to the coast and emptying into the sea. It stank of the green slime that grew over the canal walls and floated on the water's surface like filthy lace. How long ago had this water flowed past our town? Was this the snow we fetched in buckets, this the water into which Iris loved to toss only her prettiest leaves, and then to cry over losing them? Up ahead I saw a sign, BUY 'N' SELL.

The store was a narrow space, made to feel smaller by its density of objects. It was lined on both sides by glass cases, which held jewelry, watches, coins, and silver cutlery, all of it coated in dust, the dried carcasses of flies scattered about. From the walls hung weapons, tools, and instruments.

'Help you?'

The voice came from a dark corner of the room, where a man sat in a chair behind the counter, trimming his fingernails.

'I'm here to sell.'

He rolled his eyes and pressed himself to stand with great effort. He wore a dark red shirt, beneath which his chest appeared sunken and his belly bulged. 'Let's see it then.'

I unbuckled the satchel and removed the items one by one, arranging them on the glass counter. The silver candlesticks, the strand of pearls, the garnet ring. I slipped my wedding band off my finger and laid it beside these items. I brought my hand to my braid, touched the silver hairpin there, but I could not bring myself to remove it.

The man picked up each item in turn and set them down quickly and without care, as if he were not studying them to determine their value, but merely confirming their existence. Then he placed both hands on the counter. 'This is all junk.' He quoted a price, hardly anything. 'Best I can do for you.'

'But the candlesticks are silver and those are pearls. The rings are pure gold.'

He shrugged. He picked up the candlesticks again, knocked them together. 'Looks like junk to me. Anyway, nobody wants candlesticks these days. You want to sell or not?'

I stuffed the items back in my satchel and hurried out of the store.

The block was nothing but shops with signs like the first, BUY 'N' SELL, and I went directly to the next one. It, too, was a narrow room with walls crowded with weapons and tools and instruments and glass cases of jewelry and coins and precious stones. But the wares had been recently dusted, and there were no flies in the cases. It made sense that the first store in the district would not be a legitimate enterprise, that it would be there to lure inexperienced sellers and buy their things for a song. In this store, too, the proprietor sat in a dark corner, this time scratching at a patch of dry, shining skin on his arm. When I approached, he stood and I opened my satchel and laid out my items.

'This is all junk,' he said, and quoted an even lower price than the man in the first shop.

'But it's not. It's gold and silver and pearls.'

He said nothing in reply, and I gathered my things again. On my way out, glancing at the items in the glass cases, I saw that the gold looked too yellow, the precious stones too bright and glittering; they couldn't possibly be genuine. I went to the next shop, and the next, and in each shop a man seated in a dark corner picked up my items and set them down without care and offered me a price that was lower than the one before. At the final shop, a bald man with tufts of gray hair sprouting from his ears offered me the lowest price of all. I started to get angry then.

'You and I both know none of this is junk. Now offer me a fair price!' I cried.

'I already have. I run a reputable establishment. Just this afternoon I gave a man twice this sum for that cane up there. But then, that was a fine piece, solid.' He pointed to the wall above him, where a collection of animals was mounted, real animals, ones that had once been alive, a fox and a warbler and a small yellow-scaled reptile I didn't know, black marbles gleaming where their eyes should have been; beneath these, several canes hung horizontally, held by small brass hooks. The one he was pointing to was just like the man on the train's, a silver fish consuming a polished shaft.

'You're all in cahoots!' I said. 'Whatever price I'm offered at one shop, I'll always get offered less at the next. It doesn't matter what I bring you.'

The man shrugged and turned away from me. He lowered himself into his chair in the shadowy corner of the room, inserted his finger into his ear and began to excavate the wax there.

I went back to the first shop.

'Have you reconsidered?'

I laid the items on the counter without a word. But when he removed the money from the register and handed it to me, I saw he'd given me the amount I'd been offered at the last shop.

'Like I told you, it's junk,' he said before I could protest.

I took the money and ran from the shop. The bells from the cathedral were playing. It was a song I knew; we had played it at a recital in ninth. Ana had done the solo. I walked to the edge of the canal and gripped the rail and let the music come down on me from across the city, so far away it seemed possible it came all the way from our town, that I was listening to the recital for my own going. Was Iris singing now, head upturned to the clouds? I wanted to take the pittance in my satchel and buy a ticket back the way I had come. But I could not go back. Our affliction had cast its gaze upon me for a reason. It had seen something in the nature of my love for my child, something *out of balance*, and it had chosen me. And I had violated it. I should have vanished, I should be gone, but I hadn't and I wasn't, and I could not know what harm I might do if I tried to return to a place I was not supposed to be and a child I was not supposed to have. Could I even return at all? Or, the moment I crossed into the town, would our affliction sense the error of my presence there, and would the fate I had evaded be upon me? This was all I could have, all I deserved: to love Iris away from her, to spend my life elsewhere doing the labor of that love, even if it could not reach her. Maybe she would be better off this way. Maybe she would be safer from our affliction without me.

I found a little dirty-floored eatery and ordered soup with dumplings from a woman who looked aggrieved to have a customer. The broth was too rich; oil glistened in pools on its surface. The meat in the dumplings was undercooked and gelatinous on my tongue. I ate the food quickly, too hungry to reject it.

On a narrow side street a few blocks from the canal I found a hotel. It was inexpensive. I could afford three nights. My room was on the fourth floor, with a barred window overlooking the street, and the building was so poorly constructed I could hear people in the rooms to either side of mine and above and below, their heavy footsteps, their grunts on the toilet and during sex, their dry coughs. There were no children in this hotel. I stripped off my filthy clothes and washed them as best I could in the sink with a bar of cracked pink soap that sat on the counter. The water here was terribly hot and it scalded my hands. I hung the clothes to dry over a chair in the corner. I peeled back the bedspread. The sheets were strewn with hairs, corkscrews and long strands. I turned off the light so I wouldn't have to see them and slid between the sheets. I fell asleep quickly, before I could even wonder if I would be able to. I woke once, to retch the soup into the toilet, and slept a dreamless, tumbling sleep until midday.

In the days that followed, I barely left my hotel room. I had no plan for what I would do when my money ran out and I was forced to leave. I knew I ought to be making such a plan. I would need to find work and somewhere permanent to live and learn how one did everything here, how to buy food and clothes and how to get from here to there, but the scale of the tasks before me and the vanishing returns upon such efforts immobilized me. To do all of this, to learn to make my way here, and to what end?

I spent most of my days looking out the barred window. Every morning, an old man shuffled down the street beneath the weight of three black sacks. He set them down just below my window, laid an oilcloth on the sidewalk and removed a random assortment of objects from the sacks and spread them on the cloth. Socks and children's underpants, coloring books, irons, hairbrushes, wallets. He sold hardly anything, a toy boat one day, a shaving kit the next, and at dusk he packed his wares back into the sacks and departed. Around this man passed the other business of the street. Stray dogs lazed about like tossed stones. An orange tomcat slunk around, leaping from the top of a garbage pail, prowling down the alley. I saw the man from the front desk lean against the exterior of the hotel to eat his lunch, a sandwich on a hard crusty bread that shattered when he bit it, sending crumbs to his feet; when the tomcat came to eat them, the man kicked him away, and when the man had gone back inside a flock of the same dirty, rainbow-throated birds from the train station descended from the roof of the building across the street and pecked at the crumbs. Two lovers came up the street arguing, a man and a woman, pregnant. The man grabbed the woman's hand and yanked her along. They did not walk around the birds but plunged right through them, and the birds ascended in a great welter of wings. A voice yelled down from a fifth-floor window, 'Be quiet! Please, be quiet!' I saw a shopkeeper chase a man out of his store and down the street, and a man who might have been that same man, or a different one, stand in the middle of the street and shout, 'You can't stay up there forever, you crazy cunt!' Every afternoon a pack of children arrived with sticks and turned the street into a battlefield.

I left my room only twice each day. Once, to eat. They didn't sweep the streets here, and along the gutters were empty cups, candy wrappers, and some things so weather-beaten and grayed it was hard to say what they were, whether a lock of hair or a frayed knot of rope or a small dead bird. There was no shortage of dirty little eateries within a few blocks of the hotel. I tried a different spot each day and I never ventured any farther. Each eatery offered different foods, but no matter where I went or what I ate it tasted the same, excessively rich and oily, the meat fatty and undercooked, cheeses that tasted of nothing, lacking the wild flavor of our fresh cheese in town, and always the food settled in my stomach like I had eaten the lock of hair or knot of rope or small dead bird from the gutter, and always I was sick later. At one eatery, the proprietor hovered over me. 'You like it?' he asked solicitously. 'You like my food?' He had a gentle, hopeful face. I had not received such a kind look since I left town, and each time he asked I lied and told him the stew was very good, and he ladled more into my bowl.

I left my room a second time at night, to drink a tumbler of the local alcohol at the bar just off the hotel lobby. The hotel was a far cry from the Alpina. The lobby could barely be called a lobby, or the bar a bar. It was just a counter with three stools padded with ripped burgundy leather, and if you rang the greasy bell the man from the front desk would come over to serve you. I stayed just long enough to finish my drink. Back in my room, I washed my dress and underthings with the cracked pink soap, then slid between the dirty sheets. Sleep came upon me all at once, as if I had been drugged. Sometimes in the night I jolted awake. Iris had cried out. I must go to her, soothe her, I was needed. But it was only the tomcat, yowling on the deserted street.

When I went to the bar on my last night at the hotel, a man was there. When he saw me, he smiled.

'It's you,' he said.

He stared at me, and for a moment I thought he knew me, that I had been found. But he must simply mean he'd seen me before. The faces here didn't stick in my mind, they slipped right out. He smiled kindly at me, and it came to me. The eatery down the block. He must be the proprietor there, the man who had ladled stew into my bowl until I was sick for hours.

I smiled back at him. 'It's nice to see you.'

He was sitting on the middle of the three stools, so I was obliged to sit beside him. He rang the bell. When the man from the front desk arrived, the proprietor asked for a drink for me and another for himself.

'I've been waiting for you,' he said.

'I'm sorry. I didn't realize you were waiting to see me again. It's nothing personal. Nothing seems to agree with me here.'

'We'll fix that,' he said with a smile.

When our drinks arrived, he raised his tumbler. 'Cheers.'

I lifted my glass to meet his. He downed his drink in a single long sip and I followed his example, opening my throat and letting the harsh liquid rush down it. He rang the bell again. He set his hand down on the bar and let it graze the side of my own. It was the first time my body had touched another's since I arrived here, and it set off an ache inside me. I used to touch everyone, always, a thousand times a day.

When we had emptied our drinks again, I stood. 'Well, thank you. Good night.'

He picked up his empty tumbler, knocked it rhythmically against the bar. 'You don't mean that.'

I opened my mouth to protest, but he was right. I didn't mean it. Though we did things differently in our town, I knew enough to understand what he wanted, and while I didn't want it, while the thought of it repulsed and shamed me, I did want to have done it, to be repulsed by myself, and ashamed.

'Come with me,' I said.

We climbed the stairs, he in front of me; I let his movement pull me upward, and at the fourth-floor landing he stopped climbing and we made our way down the corridor to my room. We wasted no time. He removed his watch and ring and set them on the table next to the bed. He unbuckled his belt himself and stepped out of his trousers. I unbuttoned my dress and let it fall to the floor. All over my body I felt the evidence of Iris betraying me, pearly stretch marks on my belly, flattened breasts. If he noticed, he didn't care. He was soft, his penis lolled against his thigh, and I knelt beside the bed and tried to bring my mouth to him, but he turned away from me. He took care of it himself, spitting into his hand and rubbing vigorously. 'Lie down,' he said when he was ready, and in no time he was inside me. I was dry; he chafed in and out of me like my loafers against my heels. I slipped the silver pin from my hair and brought the tine to his shoulder, which was bony and covered with hairs, then brought my mouth quickly down on the blood. His hairs against my tongue were like a punishment for which I had been desperate. His blood tanged like the rusted railing along the canals. This place was in me now.

Suddenly I couldn't hear. My ears rang, a deafening sound. It took me a moment to realize what had happened, that he had slapped me. He wrenched the hairpin from my hand.

'You crazy cunt!' he shouted.

I curled in on myself in the bed, clutched the throbbing side of my face. He grabbed me, spread me apart, and shoved himself back in. As he moved in and out of me, I saw him climbing the stairs ahead of me, how he'd known to stop at the fourth floor; I'd thought nothing of it, I was used to everyone knowing where I lived. I understood then that he wasn't the kindly proprietor from the eatery at all. He was the man in the street, the one who yelled each day, 'You can't stay up there forever, you crazy cunt!' Maybe he had noticed me because of how I watched him out my window while he shouted at whomever he was shouting at, or maybe it was me he had been shouting at all along. He emptied himself with a single grunt.

He pulled on his trousers and buckled his belt. I couldn't move; I stayed naked in the bed, sheet clutched to my throat. He took his things from the bedside table, his gold watch, his ring, gold with a dark stone. I could swear it was the one I had sold the night I arrived in the city. Before leaving, he sat on the edge of the bed and pulled the sheet away from me. He took my breast in his hand, rubbed it between his thumb and forefinger. 'Junk,' he said. Then he snatched my silver hairpin from the bed where he had flung it, stuffed it in his pocket, and went out of the room.

I left the hotel at first light. I walked back across the city, past the secondhand shops and the stores selling iron bric-a-brac, hats, flowers, porcelain, the spire of the cathedral glancing in and out of view. My insides and my heels throbbed the same, rubbed and raw. When I reached the train station, I bought a ticket, after which I had only a few coins left. I rode the train for two days, as far from the city as I could go.

When the train reached the end of the line, I touched the back of my hand to the window, as to a child's forehead. The glass was cold. There were seasons here. Trees stood bereft of leaves, their branches etched against a white sky. When I debarked, I was confronted by a frigid, flapping wind. A sudden swell, I thought, and I stood on the platform and waited for it to subside, but it didn't, it was ceaseless, and eventually I stopped waiting and departed.

The cold, the wind, it was all so foreign, and yet I detected something familiar here, the quality of a place pressed against something so much bigger than itself. I had no map, but I was certain I was walking toward the sea. I could feel it pulling me as once, mere days ago, I had felt pulled into the mountains. The streets were narrow, buildings painted windswept shades, sage and blush and pale yellow. On the upper floors were apartments, clotheslines bowed across the lanes, shirts flapping in the wind. On the ground floor were pubs and cafés, but these were shuttered. I walked down lane after lane, the salt wind and pearled light telling me I was getting closer, nearly there, until I turned a corner and there it was. I stood and took it in, the biggest thing I had ever seen, a flat gray expanse stippled with white crests, out and out to a horizon to which I felt myself suddenly bound. I wanted to wish I had never seen it, but I couldn't.

The beach was a plain of ash-colored sand, before which stretched a broad, elevated walkway made of wooden planks, and I made my way there. It was nearly empty. An old man sat on a bench tossing crusts to the seabirds, mangy creatures, their feathers abraded. Another man pushed a broom down the walkway, sending clouds of fine dust into the air. Soon I reached a section lined on both sides with wooden stalls, all boarded up. The stalls went on and on, and I wondered what they had once contained, and what need there had been for so many of them in this town that was nearly unpeopled, and I shivered as I tried to imagine what had happened here. After the last shuttered stall, there was a wooden kiosk. It was open. A placard advertised coffee and cocoa and sandwiches. I ordered cheese and chutney and handed the woman behind the counter the last of my money. She took it without a word, griddled my sandwich and with a cleaver chopped it into four squares, slid them into a waxed paper packet and set it on the counter. I walked on. I was so cold that I pressed the steaming packet to my arms and cheeks to warm them before I took out the sandwich and ate. The cheese was molten, and I let it run on my fingertips and burn the roof of my mouth. But within seconds it was cold and hard. Above me, gulls turned and turned. I had no money, nowhere to go, not even a sweater to shield myself from the harsh winds of this place.

Beyond the walkway, cliffs stretched as far along the coast as I could see. Waves smashed against them and sent spray high into the air. A narrow footpath snaked up from the end of the walkway; I had no better plan than to keep moving, and I followed it, climbing up, up, until I had reached the top, where the path continued along the edge of the clifftops. A short while later I reached a spot where a second, less established path branched off from the main trail, nothing more than some trampled grass to indicate it. This second path dipped sharply down along the cliff face. The light was beginning to fade; I could no longer make out the line where sea met sky. The path quickly turned treacherous, a scramble down sharp rocks slick with sea spray. A slip, a tumble: If I fell here, the rocks and water would pound my body and carry it out, and no one would ever know it had happened, or my body would be found and no one would know who I was, and they would wonder how a woman could disappear from the world so completely that no one missed her, or came to claim her. Or maybe they wouldn't wonder. Maybe such things happened here all the time.

The path ended at a small plateau. The rock face here was hollowed out, not quite a cave, but a shelter from the wind and spray. I saw broken bottle glass and the charred remains of a fire, caught the stink of urine. In the shelter was a paper bag filled with sodden, stinking clothes and, heaped in the corner, a flannel bedroll. This, too, smelled of a person only recently departed. I wondered if he would be back. I was certain it was a man; it was the disarray, the smell, a hostile tang to it, and a dawning sense of the way the world was ordered here.

Maybe he would return to find me here and he would be angry and violent, but I was too exhausted to care. I slid into the bedroll, turning my head to breathe away from it, and fell into a sleep deepened by the pounding of the waves.

I awoke to a bright, cold day, the sun already holding place above the horizon, white against a white sky. I folded the bedroll neatly. My hair was terribly knotted and I did my best to untangle it with my fingers, then worked it into a braid. I had no mirror; I worked blindly and hoped the braid gave me a neat enough appearance, that I didn't look like what I was, a woman with no home and no place to make herself clean. The clifftop fields were wet with dew, tented in places with gossamer white webs. I stooped at the edge of the path and stroked my hands through the dead grass until they were soaking, then rubbed them against my cheeks. I walked back down the path to the walkway along the beach. Up ahead was the kiosk from which I had bought a sandwich the afternoon before. I touched my tongue to the spot on the roof of my mouth the cheese had scalded. My stomach churned, but I had no money. Much to my surprise, there was a line at the kiosk, some half dozen women, each in a dress and a sensible pair of loafers not unlike my own, their hair in tidy braids, though when I drew nearer I saw they weren't women, but girls of sixteen or seventeen. I took a seat on a bench nearby and watched as each girl in turn ordered cocoa and a bun. As they waited they chatted and laughed, and naturally I assumed they were friends. But when the last of them had received her cocoa and bun, they went around and said their names. As I was trying to sort out what they were to each other, a girl in the group called in my direction, 'Here for the fair?'

I looked at her, too dumbfounded to speak.

'Of course you are. What else would you be doing on the promenade this time of year? Come with us. Zizi did the season last year. She knows all the tricks.'

No doubt with my dress and my loafers and my braid, these girls assumed me to be their peer. The girl had spoken with such authority that I felt compelled to stand.

'I'm Ginny,' she said. 'But you can call me Gin, like the drink.'

She stared at me expectantly. She was waiting for my name, and I was inclined to lie, as I had to the man on the train. But her bright, ingenuous expression was so painfully familiar that I found myself wanting to give her the truth, as if the truth were innocent. Besides, what difference did it make? I was no one here.

'Vera.'

'Like the actress,' Gin said, and I nodded though I didn't know about any actress. 'Beats the hell out of Ginny.' She rolled her eyes at herself and the other girls laughed.

'It's a long walk. We'd better get moving,' said a girl who turned out to be Zizi.

Like that, I joined their little troop.

We walked away from the shore, toward the center of town. Not far from the train station we entered a low beige building and I found myself in a hall crowded with girls. Along the perimeter of the room were tables, behind which sat men in suits. On each table was a tented card, and the cards said things like SEAVIEW, QUEENSGATE, HOLLEMAN'S. Girls lined up at the tables and the girl at the front of each line twirled slowly with her arms above her head while the man inspected her, and then the girl held out her hands and the man examined her fingernails. I looked at my own nails, ringed with dirt.

'Zizi says Queensgate is the nicest, but they're only taking fifteen this season,' Gin said. 'I might try Holleman's first. I hear they don't mind if you don't have experience, which clearly I don't.' She rolled her eyes at herself again. She looked me up and down with what seemed both sympathy and pity. 'Good luck, Vera.' Off she dashed. Already some of the girls who had walked with us were in the lines, showing their bodies and their hands to the men behind the tables, who stroked their mustaches as they appraised the girls. At one table, a girl twirled and twirled, waiting to be told to stop, while the man blew his nose.

I fled the room for the corridor and found a bathroom, a cracked tile floor scattered with cigarette butts, the slap of bleach, the sound of running toilets. I went into a stall, sat, and released a torrent. The stall door was metal painted pea green, and initials and messages had been scratched into the paint. *L.B. eats cunts. For a good time, see Jane.* This was a school. The fair was in a caf, the tables behind which the men sat were lunch tables, which had been pushed against the walls. The girls at the fair were scarcely older than schoolgirls, likely some of them still were. I clenched the muscles in my groin and felt the soreness there. So this was what happened to girls here, this was how they lived, and life here had made them eager for this, how hopefully they twirled. I wanted to run from this place, but run to what?

I washed myself as best I could in the sink, with the blue liquid soap from the dispenser on the wall, slathering it on my arms, my neck, my armpits. The soap was harsh and drying, and it made my skin feel tight and new. With the fingernails of one hand I dug dirt from beneath the nails of the other. When I was done I appraised myself in the mirror above the sink, which was just like the one in the girls' bathroom at our school, with a thin metal edge and etchings at eye level, like a girl had tried to scratch out her reflection. The face looking back startled me.

She really could be any of the girls at the fair. I searched her, but saw no traces of a mother.

When I returned to the caf, I approached a table in a corner, behind which sat a man who looked older than the others. The line wasn't long, just three girls ahead of me, and they departed quickly, neither twirling nor showing their hands, and soon I was at the front. The tent card said STARLING'S.

'I only need one,' the man said, not looking at me. 'The early shift, five to eleven. You're not interested, so run along.'

'I don't mind early,' I said.

He looked at me. 'You're punctual? You'll arrive ready to work?'

I nodded. I held out my hands and he gave them a cursory glance.

'And you have experience?'

I closed my eyes. I nodded.

'You'll start half-time. Once the season gets going and we have more patrons, you'll get more hours. We only need one girl. You'll need stamina.'

'I have it.'

'My wife's not going to have to teach you hospital corners, remind you to dust the curtain rods?'

It was only then I understood. The men were the managers of hotels. They were hiring girls to clean rooms which now stood empty, but which, when 'the season' got underway, would be filled with people.

'I can clean anything. I'm very thorough.' I felt a keen relief, not only because the work was just this, but because for the first time since leaving home I had said a simple thing about myself and it had been true.

As I exited the hall I heard my name. It was Gin. 'I got Holleman's!' she cried gleefully as she skipped to me. 'A noon shift to boot.'

She clasped her hands around my neck and pecked me on the cheek as if we'd known each other forever. 'Did you make out okay?'

I told her I had gotten Starling's.

'I've heard that's not so bad. The noon shift?'

I shook my head. 'Mornings.'

She pressed a hand out dramatically. 'You poor thing. How will you have any fun?'

I shrugged. 'I'm up early anyway.'

'Not after a night on Wight Street,' she said mischievously. 'Never mind, you can sleep it off after your shift. Anyway, let's go. We're heading to Miss Ben's for lodging. Zizi says her rooms aren't the fanciest but they have the best beds. I don't want springs jabbing me after a night on Wight Street! Coming?' she asked when I didn't move.

'You go ahead.'

'Do you already have lodgings?'

I shook my head. 'It's just I don't have any money at the moment.'

'Not any?' She eyed me. She was picking up on something, my loafers too scuffed, hollows beneath my eyes, a few glints of silver in my braids. I had three gray hairs; I knew just where they were and once, in a life that could not possibly have been this one, I used to sit at my vanity in the middle of the day while Iris learned her letters at school and Peter examined the teeth of the town and run my fingers down their coarse, glinting shafts.

Gin took my hand. 'I'm sure Miss Ben will let you settle up after you've been paid. Let's go before she's full.'

Gin was right. Miss Ben did let me settle up at the end of the week, and in this way I came to be Gin's roommate and one of 'Miss Ben's girls' in the boardinghouse of which she was proprietress.

· · ·

The season began. The restaurants opened their doors, as did the clubs and bars along Wight Street. But the weather remained raw and blustery, and the town was still uncrowded. After my shift I would make my way to the promenade and order a cheese and chutney sandwich from the kiosk and sit on a bench to eat it. The stalls that had been boarded up when I arrived and whose purpose had been mysterious to me turned out to offer every imaginable amusement. There was a ring toss and a shooting game and darts, and games where you tried to toss a ball into a basket, a milk bottle, a fruit crate. There was a labyrinth whose walls were made of mirrors and a sort of rotating platform called the Dizzy Lizzy that spun its passengers at breakneck speed and a booth where you could dress up in bonnets and britches and stand in front of a curtain painted with an old-fashioned scene to have your photograph taken. There were food stands selling popcorn and sausages and something that didn't look like food at all, a wispy substance made in a dented metal basin. The sign said SPUN SUGAR, and one day I bought some. It looked like a cloud and tasted of sweetness, then smoke.

The promenade was still mostly empty; the few holidaymakers wandered its length as if lost and played the games in the most desultory manner. The men and women who ran the booths sat around bored, tossing popcorn into their mouths, young children asleep on thin pilled mats at their feet. Their older children roved in packs; they stabbed at crabs on the beach with shards of driftwood, spun circles until they staggered and fell to the ground. When they walked past my bench, I smiled at them, sometimes I waved and called hello, but they eyed me with suspicion and hurried past. I sat a long time after I finished my sandwich, listening to the desolate cries of gulls, the waves crashing against the cliffs, the carnival music lost to the wind. I had the impression of a great apparatus churning forward to no purpose, all of us girls with our tidy fingernails, ready to clean, the walls of the booths hung with stuffed animals and dolls, salt corroding their fur, their hair.

One day a young girl hopped onto the bench beside me. I had noticed her before. She traipsed the promenade alone, gave the other children not so much as a glance. She was skinny and sharp-kneed, with muddy white shoes, a soiled ruffled dress, a mass of untamed hair to her waist. She smiled up at me, but when I smiled back, she giggled and sprinted off. But she came back the next day, and the next. Her mother and father ran the photo booth. I saw a woman emerge from there one day and call, "Gabi! Gabi!' and saw the girl scamper over. Her mother kissed her unruly hair and then she ran off again, down to the beach, where she lunged and shouted at the gulls.

The warm weather moved in all at once. It happened at night. The wind, which had rattled the panes and sent a wailing through the eaves at Miss Ben's, died down. When I stepped out early the next morning for my shift, the air was soft against my skin. Within a week, the yellow fields along the cliffs turned green, and then they were tufted with tiny purple flowers whose name I didn't know. The days turned sunny, then hot, and the town grew more and more crowded until it seemed it could not possibly hold all the people who streamed in each day by train and car. The promenade bustled morning and night. It smelled of melted ice cream and frying oil and cigarettes. Performers of every sort jostled for the best spots: mimes and fiddlers, fire-eaters and an illusionist who could make girls levitate off the ground. We had known about seasons in our town, but I hadn't understood: How a place can become something else, how it is always both what it appears to be and the negative of what appears, that other state which hovers behind the scene like a ghost.

Starling's grew busier and my hours increased. The man who had hired me and his wife were brusque, pragmatic people. I did my job satisfactorily and they left me to myself. From the other girls at Miss Ben's I quickly picked up the hierarchy of the hotels in town, the best being Queensgate, as Gin had said the day we met. It was a white manse perched on a hill overlooking the water like a hulking seabird, with a wraparound porch where guests lazed all day sipping coffee and cocktails, and a broad lawn with white chairs where they reclined at sunset as if watching a show; they even clapped when the sun slipped below the horizon. After Queensgate came Cliff Lodge, then, Gin insisted, Holleman's, though after a few weeks in town it seemed to me that Holleman's in fact fell below Larkspur, not that I said so to Gin. Somewhere below these was Starling's. It was a small, tired inn on a shabby lane some distance from the promenade. There were eleven guest chambers and the guests were old widows and widowers alone at the sea, and transients who stayed a single night, and young families who slept crammed together in one room and kept bread and jam on top of the bureau, attracting pests.

I learned these people through the traces they left in their rooms, which it was my task to smooth away. A bedsheet twisted into a rope from a night of fitful sleep. The wastebasket beside the desk filled with crumpled drafts of a letter on hotel stationery, or with a single tissue on which a woman had blotted her lipstick. Shoes in a heap by the door, badly scuffed, the soles coming apart.

Sometimes a room was filled with a scent so like Iris's hair when it needed a wash that it leveled me. Sometimes I stepped into a room and I had the overwhelming sense that Peter and Iris had gone out from it just a moment ago, and I had missed them.

Many nights, I dreamed of return. I was in our yard behind our house on Hinter der Wald. Iris was there, barefoot in the dress from her birthday party, her small feet dewed and muddy. She plucked treasures from the grass, feathers and mushrooms and butterfly wings, and I was so happy, watching her. Then she turned to me and glared, as if I had intruded upon some private rite.

'You left me,' she said. Her voice was not that of a child. It was the accusing voice of a girl nearly grown.

'I had no choice.'

'You could have stayed until you were air.'

Now when I went to the promenade after my shift at Starling's, it was crowded. People gorged on fried fish and soda and candies, foods too sweet, too rich, too salty, yet oddly flavorless. The bins along the promenade filled with wasted food, sour and sun-warmed, and bees swarmed over them. A man shot an arrow and popped a pink balloon and whooped. A group of girls rolled up the bottoms of their shorts to show off their legs. Girls played in every configuration, in twos and threes and fours and fives; they had no need for our careful threesomes, a friend and a spare, in case one should go. Boys tramped about, squirting water pistols and filching toys and candy from the booths. One of the girls from Miss Ben's rode the Dizzy Lizzy until she vomited. A woman lifted a change purse from the back pocket of a teenage girl in front of her in the ice cream line. A man slid his hand under a woman's skirt as he passed her in the crowd. One day I saw a mother nursing an infant on a bench. As people passed, they glanced at her, and when they saw her exposed breast they sneered. A pacifier rolled out of the woman's bag onto the promenade and they saw it fall, but nobody stopped to pick it up, or even moved to avoid it, and quickly it was trampled by the crowd.

I arrived back at Miss Ben's each night in time for dinner. All the girls there worked at one of the hotels, most as maids, some as waitresses or hostesses. Nearly all of them were new to the coast, or had been here just one season before, two at most. To return for numerous seasons was shameful and reeked of failure. The goal was to involve oneself with a man here on holiday and depart with him at season's end, and to return someday as a guest instead of a maid. This was Gin's plan, the success of which she was assured of. It explained why she'd felt so sorry for me about my morning shift.

Dinner was a lively affair. Miss Ben cooked terribly heavy foods, potatoes and noodles and stews thickened with cornstarch, and the girls railed against these meals and the murder they were doing to their figures as they ate and ate, scooping food from the dishes as if trying to fill some cavity deep inside them. Around the table, they compared their jobs. They discussed the various products they deployed to improve what they all believed were their hideous complexions. They recounted their nights on Wight Street. But inevitably, the talk turned to their girlhoods. They revisited their pasts obsessively, spoke of them in breathy, aroused voices. They had all come to the coast from some nowhere or other, small villages, farms, crumbling third-rate cities, and they were proud not to have belonged in these places, proud that they required the grander setting of the coast, with its sparkling hotels and mad nights. They had left their mothers behind, mothers who had mistreated or misunderstood them, mothers who were cruel or who held them too close, and they claimed they were glad to be rid of them, though sometimes as they spoke I noticed them caressing their fingertips rhythmically over the gooseflesh of their forearms. They understood nothing, least of all themselves.

Before they went out to Wight Street, they hung around in the parlor, and I joined them there. Miss Ben always lit a fire, and the girls stood around it, warming themselves before they went out into the chilly night in their skirts and dresses. Sometimes as we stood around, I caught myself swaying, and I froze, terrified one of them had seen it. But they were too caught up in themselves to notice, and anyway, even if they had seen it, they couldn't know what it meant.

Gin went out every night, traveling the circuit of bars and clubs in her meticulously selected outfits, every hair on her head set just so with spray. Often she didn't return until it was nearly time for me to get up for my shift at Starling's. She had been right about Miss Ben's. The room was nothing special, a rough-hewn wood floor, a sink with a corroded faucet, two narrow iron bed frames with baskets beneath for our things. But the beds were comfortable, firm mattresses and stiff quilts, sheets made soft from so many washings. 'Imagine,' Gin remarked once, in that hazy hour when she was settling drunkenly into sleep and I was rousing for my day, 'how many girls have slept in these beds before you and me, and where they are now.' She said it in a dreamy voice, like she saw the mass of these girls looking back at her from some great distance, and like everything that happened to them had been good.

Sometimes I couldn't sleep at night, and from the basket beneath my bed I removed the stranger Ruth's photograph and held it up to the moonlight streaming in between the curtains. Ironic, that the only memento I had of home was a photograph of elsewhere. I would stare at the balcony and the open space paved in gray stones below, until I seemed to see past them, or through them, to Eschen and Hinter der Wald and the rushing waters of the Graubach. The town resurrected itself there, in some space behind the image on the photograph's surface. School and the skinfruit grove and the statue of the crying woman. The rooftops carpeted in moss, the moss so green it made you ache as a newborn makes you ache. All of us gathered on the lawns. The burnings and the music. The slender crack in the window of my childhood bedroom. Peter's blood. Iris's braids. They would be asleep at that hour, Peter and Iris, in our house in the town. I would close my eyes and try to feel just the tiniest ember of what it had once felt like to lie awake in our quiet house while they slept, nothing sweeter in the world. But sometimes all at once a different feeling would come over me, so heavy I thought I would be sick with it: What if I had been wrong? What if I hadn't been on the verge of going after all? What if it had all been in my mind, and I had surrendered Iris to nothing more than a fear? I would lie awake until Gin stumbled into the room and it was time for me to get ready for Starling's, wondering whether I had saved myself or thrown away my child.

Although the promenade was crowded now, Gabi always found me. At first, she did nothing but sit beside me on the bench and grin at me expectantly. When I tried to speak to her, she dashed off into the crowd. One day I offered her a square of my sandwich. She took a bite then crinkled her nose and said something I couldn't understand, because she spoke a language unfamiliar to me, which must have meant *yuck*. But I could tell she didn't really dislike it, the same as I could always tell at dinner when Iris pushed away her food. Children test you. They try your patience, yes, but I don't mean that. I mean they sound you to ascertain the limits of your openness to them. It was what Iris had done then and what Gabi, who I guessed to be about Iris's age, though she was so much scrawnier, did now.

I shrugged like I didn't care, took what remained of the sandwich from her hand and tossed it onto the promenade. Within seconds a wreck of seabirds descended, pecking and flapping at one another as they fought for the bread, tearing at it until it was nothing.

'Seagulls live by the sea and eagles live by the eag,' I said.

I knew Gabi couldn't understand these words, but she smiled.

The next day when she hopped up beside me, I offered her a square of my sandwich again, and this time she ate it happily, as if the previous day's events hadn't happened. From then on we shared my sandwich every day, after which she ran off and I spent the rest of the afternoon on the bench flipping idly through a romance novel from Miss Ben's collection, watching the people, and catching glimpses of Gabi. She stole a penknife from a boy who had stolen it from a prize wall, sprinted to the shore and hurled it into the sea. She darted in and out of the booths, often emerging with something sweet: a mint-green taffy in waxed paper, a licorice lace, a lollipop in a rainbow of twisting colors. She begged a cone of spun sugar, then peeled off wisps and held her hand aloft to let the wind take them. She hung around her parents' booth. When a girl her age took a turn in one of the puffy white bonnets, Gabi stood off to the side, crossing her eyes and sticking out her tongue as the unwitting girl smiled daintily for the camera.

She wore the same thing every day, the ruffled dress over cotton shorts and a short-sleeved shirt. The dress was a cheap garment meant for dress-up, stained and too big for her. It had pockets and she hid things in them. Sweets. Her little thefts. Smooth black stones from the shore. The tiny purple flowers that grew on the clifftops, which wilted and browned in her pockets. One day, she removed from her pocket something delicate and translucent and placed it on her palm, offering it to me. It was a butterfly's wing, a cabbage white. I reached out for it, but when I touched it, she closed her fingers over it and dashed off. I might have decided I had imagined the whole incident were my fingertips not dusted with the creature's silver powder.

I had the sense then that this child was Iris. The people here were us, looking out from the faces of strangers, disguised and forgotten to one another. My Iris was far away, growing by the day into a girl I did not know. But she was also here, hidden deep within this child, Gabi a conduit through which I might send my love to her, a stranger lit with faint traces of Iris and her life.

Every day some customers forgot to return to Gabi's parents' booth at the end of the day to claim their prints, and she stole the pictures and these, too, she stuffed in her pockets. When she hopped onto the bench she would pull them out and lay them between us. She would stare up at me expectantly and say something in her lilting tongue, the same word over and over.

'I don't understand,' I would tell her helplessly.

She would stuff the pictures back in her pocket and stomp away.

'They're twins,' I tried one day. In the photograph were two children, a boy and a girl. 'They bicker constantly, and their parents are at their wits' end.' Gabi scooted herself closer to me on the bench and settled her body against mine. This was what she had wanted, a story, even if she couldn't understand it. 'When they are twenty their parents will die in an accident and they will never speak to each other again.

They will travel to opposite ends of the earth and live separate lives, but they will both live tormented by the same problem: The love they feel for other people will never compare to the hate they felt for each other.'

Gabi looked up at me and giggled. She still had her baby teeth, small sharp points.

It became part of our routine. At first, I was tentative with my storytelling. This place was still so new to me. It was difficult to think up those things that might happen to a person here, the shape a life might take, and I felt resistant to doing so; I sensed a danger in imagining my way too fully into the lives of people here, as if I might alter myself in ways that could not be undone. I did it anyway, to win Gabi's smile, her warm body pressed to mine. She was doing this to me, changing me, drawing me closer to her and away from the other life she seemed to sense in me.

One day, the photograph was an old woman and an old man. 'They met right on this promenade sixty years ago,' I began. 'They were both singers at the lounges on Wight Street. They had a season's romance, but life drew them apart. He became a renowned performer and traveled the world. She married a boy she had never not known and only sang when she washed dishes. Last year her husband died and she sent this man a letter, and now here they are, together again. Right now, he is thinking that their coming together in old age makes sense of everything that has happened to him, his whole peripatetic existence. She is thinking that he has turned out to be a disappointment.'

'The child is a miracle.' This on another day, a photograph of a father and a mother and a boy of about eight who aimed a pistol at the camera. 'He wasn't supposed to live. He endured the most horrific medical treatments as a baby. He survived, but something was wrong.

He had endured too much, at too young an age, and his mind could not make sense of it. He is angry, and lost to them. When he is a teenager he will run away. He will stay gone for a week, and when he returns he will be kind and loving, and when he tells them he needs money they will give it to him, and in the morning he will be gone again. It will become a cycle, the running away, the sweet return, the demand, the departure. One day when he asks for money his mother will refuse, and he will shout that he has never loved her. He will touch a large dark mole on her face about which she has always been self-conscious and tell her she disgusts him. Then he will leave, and they will never hear from him again. This will nearly break them, but it won't. They will move away, to a town in the desert, and find some peace there together. It will be as if their son is dead, and the father will begin to wonder if he really did die, when he was a baby and so sick, and if the child they raised was not their son but a double sent to torment them, in which case their child was always and only the sweet, smiling baby all the nurses loved to kiss.'

'She loves horses. She lives in the city, but when she grows up she will move to the country and fall in love with a woman who trains horses. She will get everything she ever wanted, and best of all she will not question it. She will simply feel lucky and be happy.'

One day Gabi hopped onto the bench with a stuffed animal from one of the stalls in tow, an owl with giant yellow eyes. *'Ku-ru, ku-ru.'* She waved the animal through the air.

'Owls are vicious creatures,' I said evenly. 'They snatch other birds' eggs and gobble them up.'

She smiled at me.

'The eggs are baby birds. The owls eat every part.'

She reached into her pocket and held out a candy in waxed paper.

I unwrapped it and popped it in my mouth. It tasted like burnt honey and it lodged in my teeth.

'I knew a little girl once who wasn't afraid of anything, just like you,' I said. 'I told her the scariest things I could think of and she accepted them all. Her name was Iris and she was my daughter and I left her.'

Gabi looked at me and smiled.

Gin had met someone. He was staying at Queensgate for the season with his parents before returning home to take a position in his family's manufacturing firm. Home was a large city that had until fairly recently been an unglamorous industrial hub, but which, according to Gin, was 'up and coming.' She snuck away from her shift at Holleman's in the afternoons to watch him play tennis on the grass courts at Queensgate. 'I'm his good luck charm. He never drops a set when I'm there. Did you know in tennis when you've got nothing, it's called love?'

One night when she came back to our room he was with her. I kept my eyes closed and didn't move, pretending to be asleep. They fell together onto her bed. I heard the wet, smacking sounds of their kissing, then a sucking sound which I guessed was his mouth on her breast.

'So pretty, Gin-Gin,' he slurred.

'Sshhh,' she scolded. 'You'll wake her up.'

I heard unzipping and unbuckling, shoes dropping to the floor, the whisper of Gin's dress slipping off. I heard skin rubbing against sheets, springs creaking, and I tried to hear past it to the other night sounds. A toilet flushing and water rushing through the pipes. Snatches of raucous conversation from people stumbling home on the street below. The distant song of a street musician on Wight, so faint I couldn't be sure it was really there. As soon as they were finished, the boy hurried into his trousers. 'You're the best, Gin-Gin,' he said, and with a kiss he was gone, though his scent lingered, semen almost floral in its perfume, and so thickly laced through the stagnant air in our room that I took it into myself with every inhalation. While Gin snored in her bed, so near to me I could almost reach out and touch her, I thrust my hands down under my nightgown and tried to imagine that my hands were Peter's hands, that the warmth of my bed was his warmth, and that this smell was his, and for a moment my mouth filled with the taste of his blood. But I couldn't hold on to it long enough, couldn't take myself to the edge with it. I finished myself not out of desire but compulsion, and my climax was pleasureless, the torture of wanting, the collapse into *getting*, but getting what? A need met, a thing taken care of, nothing more than an occurrence and an end.

'Did I wake you last night?' Gin asked innocently over the dinner table the following evening.

I told her she hadn't, and from then on the boy from Queensgate came home with Gin most nights and had sex with her in her bed, after which he departed and I tried and failed to hold on to Peter long enough to come as if he had made me come. In the near-darkness I dressed and went to my shift at Starling's. Then the promenade, and Gabi. One day I gave her a few coins to play the games and she won a doll small enough to fit in her hand, with a wafer-thin pink dress, black shoes that were painted on and eyes that didn't close. After, we sat together on the bench and she held the doll in one hand and banged it against the bench.

'Poor dolly,' I said.

From then on, the doll lived in her pocket. Sometimes she took it out and I saw her chewing on its hair.

. . .

One afternoon, I saw a woman walking along the promenade with a basket swinging from the crook of her arm. It was one of ours. A single dark cord ran through the center of the handle. Ana had made it. Her fingers had touched those vines. I wanted to run to the woman and snatch the basket for myself, but of course I didn't; that was the sort of daring thing Ana would do, only Ana would never have been here to do it, because Ana would never have run. I thought of her back in our town, raising her children and continuing on as she always had, passing my Iris on the street or in the park, maybe pausing to fix her braid or to tell her to button her sweater, seeing her all the time like it was nothing, and the thought of this didn't hurt or shame me as I might have expected it to, but provided a queer solace. I sat on my bench and watched the woman with the basket draw away from me until she disappeared into the crowd.

First the nights grew colder, then the days. People walked the promenade in pullovers. Children emerged from the sea and stood chattering and violet-lipped as their parents wrapped them in towels and rubbed them down. The sea itself changed, the sparkling blue yielded to a gray like the pencil smudges I used to make at the edges of my notebooks. I had the feeling of a great happening undoing itself piece by piece.

Like Gin, many of the girls at Miss Ben's had met someone. The season was more than halfway gone, and the rest of it would pass in an instant, though it was my first season and I didn't know that yet, hadn't yet learned the way time passed here. At dinner the girls spoke exuberantly of their plans, the cities they would move to at season's end, where they hoped to find work at beauty counters and live in boardinghouses of much higher quality than Miss Ben's for the brief time until these boys asked them to marry them. Gin's boy hadn't asked her to go with him yet. 'I don't push him,' she said to me after dinner one night, away from the other girls. 'That's why he hasn't asked me yet, but he will. The other girls push and I know better.' She was often sick these days, after her nights on Wight Street, though I noticed she was no longer drunk, and I wondered if the boy had noticed, too.

When the season did end and the guests traveled back to their cities, it turned out that many of the girls' plans had changed. They now claimed to have heard that the jobs in the city paid terribly and the boardinghouses were filthy. They had decided to go home after all. Gin's invitation from the boy at Queensgate never materialized. She didn't tell me this. I knew because she said nothing. She, too, had decided to return home. She said nothing about her sickness, either, and when we said goodbye, she embraced me and said cheerfully, 'See you next summer, maybe?' though there were tears in her eyes. We promised to write each other, but we never did.

The next day I collected my last pay from Starling's. When I went to the promenade, Gabi wasn't there. The booths were boarded up, and I walked the promenade as I had walked it several months before, astonished at how the passing of the season, the turning of the town from one thing to another and back, seemed to wipe away everything that had happened.

Miss Ben and I came to an agreement. I could stay on in my room in exchange for keeping the house and managing repairs during the off-season. She was getting old and the work exhausted her. 'Besides,' she said, 'you don't cause problems.'

With the pay I had managed to save from Starling's, I went to the photo shop in town and purchased a camera, an inexpensive model with a mediocre lens. In my room at Miss Ben's, I stored it in the basket under the bed that had been Gin's. The wind was back. It rattled the window as if desperate to get in.

I stayed years by the sea. I watched the seasons come and go. The brewing gray skies, the biting salt wind, the desolate promenade. Sometimes I could walk the length of it and see no one, and I would become convinced that everyone but me had gone, that here, too, it was possible to vanish, and I alone remained. Just when I had forgotten the warm season, quit believing it had ever been real, the weather softened, the winds flailed and died like a candle sputtering out, the shuttered hotels and bars and carnival booths opened and soon it was hot and the ocean sparkled, and the town was so densely peopled, so bursting with life it seemed it could not possibly end.

In the cold season I had time. The task of maintaining Miss Ben's required only a few hours each day when it was just us two tidy, quiet creatures living there. I spent much of the rest of my time with my camera. I photographed the clifftops, images framed so that the edge, the drop, was just out of view, so you might be looking at a harmless meadow nowhere near the sea. A spiderweb over soaked blades of grass. Driftwood in the sand, silver and feather-light. The sea itself: the white chop, the brown froth that washed ashore, and the flat expanse of it, on and on, which to the naked eye appeared all surface, but which in photographs carried the weight of its concealed depths.

I was never not photographing our town. It seemed that other world was locked away, held captive within this one. If only I attended to just the right detail I might summon it, free it. Then Gabi might shed her skin and Iris would run to me. At times it seemed to hide itself everywhere, to press so near. Though I knew how far off it truly lay, that it was now, for me, elsewhere.

Sometimes I swam in the sea. I waited until the season's end, when the beach was empty and the air had cooled but the sea had not. I shed my clothes at the top of the beach and walked down to the water in my swimsuit, cold sand beneath my feet. At first I stepped in just a little ways, let the waves lap at my ankles. A memory would come to me then of my feet in the shallows of that other water, the Graubach, my toes wriggling next to Peter's toes back when we were just two shy children side by side, and the life we would make together was still unknown to us, and so was its end. Then I would dive in. I would swim out, out, until I tired. I would close my eyes and float on my back, bobbing in the warm, salt-thick sea, and if I could lose myself enough in that motion, it would seem that this was that other, original sea, that I was inside my mother waiting to be born. Everything that had happened to me had been a dream, a forewarning, and when she expulsed me I would begin to live this life again from the start, and always it would take me exactly here, to this warm sea where I closed my eyes and floated and waited for it to begin.

Every season, Gabi's family returned. When they arrived she was always pale, her skin dry and ashen. I watched her grow up this way, in cycles of contracted presence followed by long spans of absence. For a brief time each year we belonged to each other, then she left the sea tanned and was gone for months, and the Gabi who returned was not the Gabi who had left, but a paler, older girl, who carried within her a world I couldn't see and could only guess at by the changes in her.

One season, the dirty dresses were gone. In their place Gabi wore cutoffs and oversize shirts. She still wore her hair to her bottom, unbrushed and cured by the salt water into crackly cords. She still stole from the older boys who stole and caused all kinds of mischief on the promenade that left people scratching their heads. I was the only one who knew it was Gabi who did these things, who stole a spun sugar cone for a girl whose parents refused to buy her one, who went along the shore finding cameras in beach bags and switching them with identical cameras in other beach bags while the families swam, who parted the curtains at her parents' booth just enough to insert herself into the photos without being seen, though the customers would surely notice sometime later, when they returned home and took the photos out and saw how the backdrop wavered slightly, and in the slit between the two panels: a tongue, an eye.

The next season she joined the boys, wreaking havoc everywhere, getting shooed away by the same proprietors who had offered her treats the season before, exchanging brags and taunts with the boys, for she had by then learned to speak the language spoken here. But she and I continued our habit of speaking across one another in our native tongues. She still took the time to sit with me on our bench each afternoon and share our sandwich, and sometimes after she ate, she lay with her feet planted on the bench and her knees pointing up at the sky and her head in my lap. She was perhaps eleven years old, a hardened little thief one minute, a tender child the next, naming the shapes she saw in the clouds.

Sometimes, when she laid her warm head in my lap, I gathered her hair in my hands and closed my eyes and braided it by feel. I made myself forget that she was Gabi, and briefly, briefly, for I couldn't sustain it long, I gave myself the feeling of my child's hair against my fingertips. I hoped that maybe, somehow, my touch might reach across the distances and Iris might feel it in her own long hair, even if she didn't know it was me, even if she thought it was just the clouds, weighting themselves there.

One afternoon after Gabi ran off, a gull landed on her spot on the bench to peck at the crumbs she had left behind. I looked into its translucent yellow eye and urged it to fly to our town and tell Iris I was here, loving her from this place, and I would never stop, before we shot it down and drowned it.

More seasons passed, and one year when Gabi returned she was transformed. Just the season before she had been a scrawny child. Now she had hips and breasts, and she had grown taller than me. She still wore cutoffs and an oversize short-sleeved shirt, but now she knotted the bottom of the shirt to expose her navel. It was just her father and her. Her mother wasn't there.

'Mama?' I asked, in both of our languages because the word was the same.

She said something, and I shook my head to show I didn't understand.

She said the same word again, then raised a hand to her neck and made a slicing motion, and I knew the word must mean, *Dead*.

When I tried to take her hand in mine she jerked it away.

She left the boys behind that season for a group of girls, the daughters of other proprietors along the promenade. These girls had been there all along, but Gabi had ignored them, or they had rejected her, I couldn't be sure. Now, though she still sat with me some days, and shared my sandwich and even, a few times, settled her head in my lap, most of the time she strutted past me, arms linked with the arms of these girls. They climbed to the top of the cliffs and sat at the edge, smoking into the salt spray and brushing each other's hair.

• • •

That season, there was a girl at Miss Ben's from the same town as Gin, and over dinner one night I asked if she knew her. I cooked the dinners myself now. Miss Ben's joint pain prevented her, though she was unwavering about what to cook, and I prepared the same starchy foods as ever.

'You know *Ginny*?' the girl asked with a smirk. 'Total sad case.' She wasn't speaking to me anymore but holding forth to the other girls around the table. 'Three children with different fathers. You never saw a woman so unkempt. None of her clothes have ever seen an iron, and her *hair*, flakes all stuck in it with grease. Honestly, the way some women let themselves go.'

The other girls shook their heads, mystified that a woman who had once been one of Miss Ben's girls would allow this to happen to her. The conversation moved on, and the girls pounced on the next topic just as ravenously, shoveling food into their mouths all the while.

Every year brought the same cycles, the same seasons and people, yet slowly the way it appeared to me shifted. I was learning this place, attuning myself to the meaning people here found in it. Now when I watched the people on the promenade, the couples playing like children at the carnival games, the packs of boys enacting their violence, mothers walking blithely with their children, I tried to remember how they had appeared to me that first season, so shallow and crude, but I couldn't quite get there. Instead, I was overcome with tenderness toward them. How small their lives were, how little they amounted to, and still they put forward these acts, private graces that contributed to nothing beyond themselves, and which increasingly seemed to me to possess an agonizing sweetness.

Every season I was another year older than the girls at Miss Ben's, which allowed me to see more clearly how young they really were. I would sit at dinner and listen to them prattle about the virtues and deficits of various night creams or haunts along Wight Street, and I could feel their desperation to believe that these things might give them the lives they wished for, and an urge would seize me to run my fingers through their hair the way I used to with Iris when some hurt brought her to my arms. I would look around the table, girl to girl to girl, and think how they would never have to face the peril the girls in our town had known, and how innocent they were. And their innocence did not seem like a limitation; it was precious.

One season, I had a lover. He was much older than me, a guest at Starling's who had rented a room for the season. Before I ever saw him, I learned from servicing his room that he was an artist. He kept his supplies on the desk, lined up in a way that suggested to me they had been set down with great care: a box of pencils, vine charcoal, gray kneaded rubber erasers, a pad of thick deckle-edged paper. I opened this and leafed through it. Quick, gestural sketches. Gulls above the sea. The clock tower in the center of town. A woman, over and over, drawn from behind, hair gathered at her nape, just the hint of a profile, a single flicking stroke for eyelashes, a gash for the edge of a long neck.

The first time we met, he was returning to his room as I was leaving it. I couldn't believe he was the artist. His hands were so large and looked so graceless. He invited me to dinner at a little restaurant on a narrow backstreet where we ate a delicious stew, after which he asked me back to his room.

I had not been with anyone since that horrible night in the hotel in the city years before. I couldn't remember the last time I had even touched myself, it must have been years ago. That first season I had touched my-self incessantly, every night after Gin's boyfriend left, desperate to feel what Peter had made me feel, but after so many nights spent trying, the feeling of my own pleasure had turned sour and tedious, just more mus-cle, more nerve, more body, hardly different from chewing my tongue.

In a bed at Starling's I had made myself earlier that day, I discov-ered the intimacy of strangers. Hands that didn't know me or what I liked or what I wanted and which moved over my body like strange-ness itself. Could he tell that I had birthed a child? Had he and the woman from his sketches had a child of their own? I didn't ask and I never found out. After we had sex, we read and laid about and drank coffee. We talked only about what was right before us. We never asked one another about the past, the lives that had led us here, and for long stretches we said nothing at all. Peter and I had never been silent to-gether, we were always going over this or that; there was so much to say, a whole life to keep on track. With this man I was reminded of my father, the silence one shares with a person who is like you, and who, because they are like you, is a mystery to you.

I was happy that season. For the first time since I left our town I allowed myself to think that maybe this place, too, could offer me a life. I could take what was available to me here and let myself become a person of this place and live and love as people here lived and loved and the things that happened to me here might be, nearly, enough.

As the season neared its end, we floated ideas. I could come with him. He lived simply, in an old farmhouse in the country; there was a spare room I could convert to a darkroom if I wished. Or he could write to his brother, tell him to find a buyer for the house, and we could purchase a little apartment together in one of the buildings along the backstreets here. We really thought we would do this. I saw us so clearly, together in a bed beside a crackling fire as the winds of the cold season wailed and snow fell into the sea.

But when the season ended we still hadn't settled upon a plan, and gradually we came to understand that this had been by design on both of our parts, and he returned to his home and I returned to my room at Miss Ben's. What bound us was also the reason our bond proved too frail to endure; it was the lesson our lives had taught us, one we had learned too well: You do not get to keep what is sweetest to you; you only get to remember it from the vantage point of having lost it.

The season after that, I hardly saw Gabi. Or rather, I saw her from a distance, but she rarely stopped to sit with me. She didn't wear cut-offs anymore but jeans that flared at the bottoms, and cropped white blouses with puffy short sleeves, tied her hair up in matching white scrap. She was with the boys again, only now she was with them differently. She sat beside a boy at the water's edge, bare feet twining together; the boy took a mound of chewing gum from his mouth, pulled it until it snapped, and placed half in her mouth with his unclean fingers. One morning on my walk to Starling's, I saw her stumbling back from Wight Street, a boy, not the one she had been with at the shore, wrapping his arm around her waist. She smoked cigarettes and exhaled into their faces, dove into the surf on the days when it was rough, trying to make herself dangerous to them, but they knew there was nothing for them to fear in her. They passed her among themselves. Now her hair went unbrushed again, and I saw all the boys' hands in it, pulling and squeezing that hair she had rested, not so long ago, in my lap.

I tried to talk to her. 'This isn't you, Gabi,' I said on one of the rare occasions when she came to sit with me.

'How would you know?' It was the first time she had ever spoken to me in my language, and in this tongue she seemed to become a different girl, spiteful and sharp. She tore a shard of bread from her sandwich and tossed it on the ground at our feet.

I was pathetic to her in this moment, trying to advise her, to mother her. For years she had taken my love; now she tossed it back at me, and I let her do it. Maybe it was Iris, loving me with her scorn across our distances. What did she look like now? What did she love? If she passed by me right now, on this promenade, would I even know it was her? Soon she would be an upper, and then?

'I'm always here for you,' I said weakly.

Gabi rolled her eyes. 'Great.' She flung the remains of her sandwich on the promenade and stalked off.

'I love you,' I called to her back.

The gulls massed around me, and I sat motionless as they devoured the bread.

The next season, Gabi's father returned alone. When I asked where she was, he only shook his head sadly. I lingered in town a short while. But every day it became clearer to me that with Gabi gone I had no reason to stay. I gave my notice at Starling's and paid out the month at Miss Ben's. I walked to the train station and boarded a train bound for a city in the desert. I stayed there several months, photographing its sage hills and dry riverbeds and its sky, which appeared entirely disconnected from the earth beneath it, viscous and flashily blue like the liquid soap we had used to scrub dishware at Starling's. I recognized the beauty of this place without loving it, as one recognizes without loving the beauty of all places one passes through too briefly to claim them or be claimed by them. I traveled next to a village in the vast agrarian plains. Every photograph I took there was a panorama; I couldn't stop trying to capture the feeling of it, on and on, so much flatness that if you had lived there your whole life and known only this place, and someone came to you and told you that in other places the land rose into the clouds, you could not possibly believe them. From there, I boarded a ship across the sea to a city I had learned about from the girls at Miss Ben's. Many of them had dreamed of ending up in this city, which was famous for the dazzling clarity of its light, and it was as stunning as everybody said: the climate dry and sunny, the land burnished, the leaves on the trees golden green.

I moved from place to place and I saw many things. I found odd jobs, cleaning or washing dishes. Sometimes in cities I rented time in a darkroom and printed images of these places to which I would never return. By all appearances I was living the life I had feared would be mine when I was a girl: childless, a spinster, moving about in the red glow of a darkroom. I was nothing but Vera. I went where I went and my movements and actions signified nothing, portended nothing, and the years accrued rather purposelessly, their only meaning that they were mine.

I had been traveling this way for several years, and had grown into this life and its transience, when I chose as my next stop a region known for its lakes, the reaching of which required a connection through the terminal in the large city in the interior where, years before, I had spent three nights hidden away in my hotel room among the canals.

When I stepped off the train and walked into the concourse and looked up, the glass dome was sparkling clean. The sky slipped right through it, filling the space with fresh light. I leaned against a wall and watched the people hurrying in every direction. Gone were the lost-faced men and agitated women from my first time here. The undistinguished masses in their drab clothing had been replaced by brighter crowds. I saw students with leather bags flapping against their sides; women striding across the floor in pumps, coats cinched fashionably at their waists; a raucous group of children on a school trip, here, no doubt, to see the cathedral. The terminal had become an airy, functional place filled with benign people, devoid of the menace that once pervaded it. No, it occurred to me. The people hadn't changed. It must have been just this way last time, too, the same mix of workers and students and tourists, a few old men and women plodding across the concourse with their canes, gossamer white hair rising from their scalps.

I had three hours before my connecting train, and I had not planned to leave the terminal; I wanted nothing to do with this city. But now I couldn't resist seeing whether my experience at the terminal would hold in the blocks along the canals, where elsewhere had so brutally taught me its rules, and I found myself going out of the terminal and heading that way. I could smell the canals before I reached them, the tamed, shunted waters of the Graubach languishing in the locks like a caged creature, a tangy smell like cold blood. Everything was just as I remembered it: the corroded railings, the trash along the streets flattened and drained of color, the alleys with their cramped, harshly lit eateries. The secondhand shops were still there. So, too, was the hotel; that window there had been mine. This had been a bleak warren and it still was, but I found that it held no power over me now. It was only a place, and I had been so many places, and I was not the frightened young woman I had once been here. I still had plenty of time before my train and I decided that I ought, at last, to visit the cathedral.

I walked north. Within minutes I had crossed out of the canal district into a residential neighborhood. The spire of the cathedral was visible now. I was entering the elegant enclaves adjoining the central district where the cathedral and the museums and the seat of government were located. The streets were lined with stone buildings with iron balconies and white shutters, window boxes with petunias draping down, ivy creeping up the walls. The noonday bells began to toll. I was near enough that the peals set my body trembling, and the scene around me seemed to waver slightly, as if it were painted on a thin curtain. Up ahead the rows of buildings lining the narrow street yielded to a wash of light. I think I knew already what I would find there, and when I reached it and the buildings fell away and the city opened up around me, gray below and gray above, I had the uncanny sense that I had stepped into a place from a forgotten dream. I was standing in the plaza from the photograph left behind by the stranger Ruth.

I laid my suitcase on the sidewalk, unfastened the clasps and removed the photograph from where I always kept it, tucked among my own prints in a leather folio. Holding it up to the scene before me, there could be no doubt. The photograph had been taken from a balcony, through the intricate wrought iron rail, and it was possible to match the ironwork to a single building on the plaza's eastern length. Visible in the photograph was a porcelain garden stool I'd never paid much attention to, with a stylized landscape of mountains and clouds and vines heavy with blossoms. I looked at the building and there it was, the very same object, on the balcony of the middle unit on the third floor. I walked across the plaza and stood beneath the building, staring up at the balcony. I had the sense then that when I fled our town, I hadn't slipped loose of my fate as I had believed. I had been following it all along, traveling toward this place whose image was the only thing I had carried with me everywhere.

I opened the heavy wood door and stepped inside. The interior of the building was stately but faded, a black-and-white tile floor, white scratches on the black tile, black scuffs on the white. A narrow stair-case, its marble steps dipped at their centers from decades of footsteps. Did she swim? Did she drown? I climbed quickly, suitcase banging against my side, and arrived on the third-floor landing breathless. When I knocked, the door opened at once, as if she had been waiting for me. But the woman who stood in the doorway wasn't Ruth. She was a plain-faced woman, older than me; she wore beige slacks and a stiff white blouse, house slippers on her feet.

'Can I help you?' She spoke with the flat accent common in the villages to the south of the city.

'I'm not sure. I'm looking for a woman who used to live here.'

She shook her head. 'You must have the wrong apartment.' She began to close the door.

'This would have been a long time ago. Maybe you have some in-formation on the people who lived here before you?'

She looked startled. 'Oh, no, I don't own the apartment. I'm the housekeeper. But my employer has lived here his whole life. He was born in this apartment.' She gestured with her hand toward the interior. Past the foyer with its gleaming parquet floors I could see the parlor, which was neat as a pin, for this woman was good at her work, and beyond it a small back room.

'Then he must know the woman I'm looking for. Her name was Ruth.'

The woman shrugged. 'I've worked here eight years and I've never heard about any Ruth. Now if you'll excuse me.'

'I really am sorry to bother you,' I pressed on. 'But I have this pic-ture.' I held it out to her. She studied it dutifully but without interest. 'Wouldn't you say it was taken from this apartment?'

She pursed her lips. 'Hard to say. The view from all of these apartments is nearly identical.'

'But look at the garden stool. You see, I'm certain she was here. It was this apartment, not any of the others.'

I heard the sound of a chair being pushed back deep in the apartment, and footsteps approaching through the brightly lit rooms. The woman heard the sounds, too, and glanced nervously behind her.

'Please, ma'am,' she said urgently. 'You've got to go now.'

But her employer had already reached the door. 'Do we have a visitor, Judith?' he asked. He turned to look at me, and though he had aged, and his hair had grayed and lost its shine, I would have known him anywhere.

'This lady is looking for a friend of hers, some Ruth, but I've assured her no such person has ever lived at this residence. She'll be on her way now. I apologize for the disturbance.'

'Vera,' Mr. Phillips said. 'How wonderful to see you again.'

He led me to the parlor and gestured to a wing back chair upholstered in red and gold damask. He lowered himself onto the sofa. We sat silently facing each other for a moment as Judith clattered about in the kitchen. She whisked in with a lacquer tray and laid out tea and shortbread on the table between Mr. Phillips and myself.

'The stranger who visited us when I was a girl took a photograph from your balcony. She was here,' I said after Judith left the parlor.

He nodded.

'We thought she stumbled upon us by accident, but she didn't. She knew about us from you. She lived here, with you?'

'For a time. That was well before Judith's day. I don't want you to think she was being deceitful. She's absolutely upstanding.' With a pair of silver tongs, he dropped two sugar cubes into his tea.

'Was she your housekeeper before Judith?'

'Ruth was never in my employ.'

'Then you were lovers?'

'Lovers,' he repeated with a light, dismissive laugh, as if he were not the sort of person to whom the term could apply. 'We were very fond of each other. I told her not to go to the town. I warned her.'

'Did you see her again, after she left us? Did she return?'

He lifted a small silver spoon from the tray and stirred the sugar into his tea slowly. 'I'm afraid not.'

I saw the stranger Ruth in the outfit I had loved best, the crepe dress with the white flowers in which she came to us, the straw hat with the ribbons, the soft brown boots. I heard the sounds of her pleasure in our house at night, saw the emptiness in her eyes as she watched the burning. 'She couldn't understand us,' I said finally.

'Quite right, my dear.'

It was hard to think clearly, with the shock of seeing Mr. Phillips. But something was nagging at me, something that did not come together, and finally I found the words for it. 'You don't seem surprised to see me.'

'Don't I? Well, it's a wonderful surprise, as I said. Simply wonderful.'

I took a tea bag from the lacquer tray. The paper wrapping was pale blue, with an illustration of tea leaves embossed in gold. 'It's the same we had in town. I haven't seen it out here, not all this time.'

'A small purveyor. I buy half their stock for the towns I supply, and the rest stays in teahouses around the city. I take it you didn't settle here?'

I shook my head. 'I was here very briefly in the beginning. It was so difficult in the beginning.'

'But you look well, Vera. It suits you here.'

I felt ashamed then. I had never wanted it to suit me here. 'You still go there? You're still running the supply?'

He took a shortbread from a china dish and chewed with his mouth neatly shut. 'I'll retire soon. But for now, yes.'

I shifted forward in my seat. 'Then you see them. You see Iris and Peter.'

He nodded.

'Tell me.'

He sipped his tea, set it on a coaster on the table so delicately it didn't make a sound. He folded his hands in his lap. 'I'm afraid I can't.'

'What do you mean? Please, I want to know everything.'

He inhaled slowly. 'As you're aware, I perform my duties with the utmost discretion.' He glanced toward the kitchen to be sure Judith wasn't listening. 'I never speak of the town to anyone elsewhere.'

'But I'm not somebody elsewhere.'

'Aren't you?'

'Please, Mr. Phillips. I have to know. Can't you understand that? If you'll just tell me what's become of them I'll go. I won't ever bother you again.'

He pressed a white napkin to his lips. He smiled amusedly. 'You're not bothering me. As I've said, it's lovely to see you, and looking so well. One thing I suppose I can say, since it's concerning a past we share, is that I was always especially fond of you. I try not to be partial, but I suppose one can't help one's preferences.' He looked into my eyes and let out a light, contemplative laugh. 'Remarkable. Iris looks so very much like you and yet. . . .'

'And yet what?'

'Forgive me. A slip. It's just I do worry for Iris. I suppose worry can make a person careless.'

'Why do you worry?'

'Vera.'

It seemed to me as if Iris were locked away in the next room, just on the other side of the parlor wall with its blue toile paper, and he had the key in his pocket and wouldn't give it to me.

'You have to tell me. What do you mean, you worry for her? Does she seem . . .'

'Vulnerable?'

I nodded.

'I really do apologize. I've said far more than I should have. Best to just put it out of your mind. And look, you haven't touched the shortbread. Please, eat. Judith will think they weren't to your liking.' He lifted the lacquer tray from the table and held it out to me.

All these years away from my child, I had consoled myself that I was doing what I must, that I was not meant to have her, and I had hoped that my absence might be what she needed, that it might protect her. And still, and yet . . .

'I have to go back.'

Mr. Phillips sighed and set down the tray. 'You mustn't. You can't.' He spoke these words in a peculiar, rote way.

'But if it's as you say, if Iris seems at risk . . .'

'An understandable impulse, but I cannot recommend it.' He leaned forward and set a hand on my knee. 'You're not supposed to be there, my dear.' He spoke gently and stroked his fingertips lightly, lightly, against my knee. Yet I couldn't shake the sense that his concern was not really for me, for us, that there was some other reason he wished

to keep me away, something he didn't wish for me to see, so that although he spoke with tender concern, I heard his words as a threat.

'You're very welcome to stay here, Vera. There's a spare bedroom
just down that corridor. Judith puts on a stern front, but she's a wonder, truly. You're welcome here as long as you like.'

'I won't stay.'

He dropped his hand from my knee. 'I urge you to think carefully
about what you're doing.'

I stood. 'Good day, Mr. Phillips. Please thank Judith for the tea.'

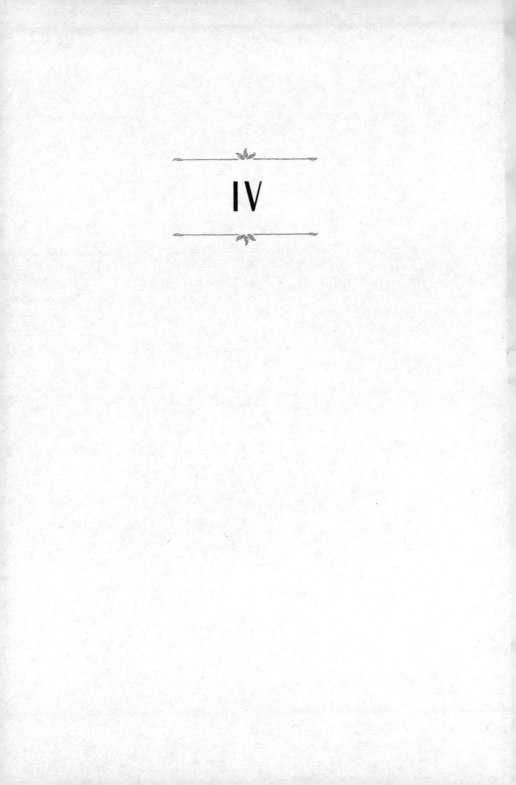

IV

Once I fled along this route. Now I retraced my steps. The train was crowded. I found an open seat in a compartment with a mother and father and their three boys, who climbed the seats and bickered over three lollipops, each boy claiming the red one. When the train began to pull slowly away from the terminal, I pressed my face to the greasy window and watched the spire of the cathedral I still had not visited grow smaller and smaller until I could no longer make it out. The train picked up pace. The city gave way to its desolate peripheries which gave way to jungle. The parents and the boys disembarked, and at once I was so utterly alone in the compartment I wondered if I had imagined them. At every stop many people got off and few got on, and the train lightened and quietened as it made its way deeper into the jungle until it seemed I was the only one left. I had the strange notion then that this train existed only for me, that it had traveled this route empty of passengers for years, waiting for the day I would step aboard.

When it reached the last settlement before the supply road, I debarked and continued on foot. I walked along the tracks. Through the steaming thickets, underbrush whipping my ankles, spindly branches snagging my hair. Animals called from the trees, and they seemed to speak to me, but whether they said *Come*, or *Turn back*, I couldn't determine.

I traveled for hours, lost track of time altogether. I was certain I should have come upon our supply road long ago, and I began to fear that our affliction had concealed it from me, that I had walked right past it and seen nothing but jungle. Just when I was starting to panic that I really could not go back, that I could travel these tracks forever, searching for a way to return, and the way would never reveal itself, it appeared, ordinary as anything: a smooth dirt path that met the tracks and traveled steeply and sinuously away from them, up into the mountains.

Evening was swiftly approaching, the clouds would be gathering, but I made slow progress, unaccustomed to the exertions of so steep an ascent. I kept my eyes on the ground, watching out for roots and stones. When at last I reached the final crest and glimpsed the pitched roofs of town, my eyes filled with tears. For years I had conjured these rooftops from the depths of the stranger Ruth's photograph, dreamed of this sight. I hesitated then. If I was to vanish, would it happen here? I looked back down the length of the supply road. It wasn't too late to turn around. I could take a train to a city I had never seen before and that meant nothing to me and try to forget what Mr. Phillips had said. But I couldn't turn away. They were right here, Peter and Iris and her need, whatever Mr. Phillips kept from me, and if I lost myself in the reaching of her, so be it, for I was too near to resist.

I looked down at my feet. I shuffled by the smallest increments toward the bound where the supply road's packed earth met the cobbles of Bergstrasse. I stretched my arm out in front of me, wriggled my fingertips in the air. No force blocked me, and my hand did not fade mirage-like into the clouds. I stepped without difficulty onto the street.

I walked slowly down Bergstrasse. It was empty. They had all retreated inside. As I walked, I scanned my body: feet, eyes, mouth, skin, checking for the sensations that had assailed me in my final days in town. But I felt right as rain. Music floated from the open windows, children in parlors practicing their instruments before dinner, small hands rosining bows and stretching to reach chords on pianos, 'Hot Cross Buns' on a wooden recorder. They looked up when I passed, but they were too young to have known me, and when they saw me they simply stared, stunned.

I wanted to run to the house on Hinter der Wald, but I was so afraid. Peter might have a new wife now, Iris a mother, the only one she thought she needed. What would I say for myself, faced with them? That I had run from them, but now I expected them to welcome my return? Besides, it wouldn't do to turn up like this, on the edge of night, disarrayed from my long journey. I needed a place to stay the night, and I walked down the streets, moving in the direction of the Alpina.

The town was not as I remembered it. Everywhere I saw evidence of ill repair: sidewalks crumbling and overtaken by weeds, tin pails set out on porches to catch leaks, eaves thick with birds' nests, the wood boards beneath spackled with their gray and yellow droppings. I passed a house with a rooftop carpeted with moss and for a moment I saw only that pure green, a color I had missed in my bones, so saturated it seemed to breathe into the air; but the roof warped under the weight of it, and the wood shingles beneath it were the unmistakable black of decay. In yard after yard, wet clothes hung limp on lines where they would not dry, and everywhere I breathed in the sour smell of dampness too persistent to tame, the tang and curdle of wet wood, wet linen, so that even as tears rolled freely down my cheeks—I was home, I was back, in this place for which I had grieved and longed—I was forced to raise my hand to my nose to shield myself from a stench that must have been there all my life.

I turned onto Hauptstrasse. I passed the bakery, the grocery, the sporting goods store where Rapid had been. When I reached the Alpina I went in, and at the reception desk I found myself face-to-face with Marie. How happy I was in that moment, how sweet it was to see her after all this time. She looked well. Her face had remained smooth and unwrinkled, and her expression still retained the bright translucence of youth, though perhaps it was simply that I still saw the girl she had once been in the woman who stood before me now. She clasped her hands and settled them on the desk between us. The bracelet on her wrist clinked against the wood. She cleared her throat.

'You'll have to excuse my nerves,' she said. 'We haven't had a guest here in quite some time.'

I stood there a moment, not understanding. My eyes were drawn again to the bracelet on her wrist. It was mine, my gold bangle with the red stones.

'Marie?'

Her lips parted and she stood unmoving, stricken. Then she broke into a nervous laugh and brought a hand to her lapel and touched the small white pin there, on which her name was printed in gold letters. 'Always forget I have this on. Yes, that's right, I'm Marie. I'm manager here. Lucky you came now and not last year. Management was a nightmare before I took over. But I've got everything in tip-top shape. Now how can I help you? I assume you'd like a room.'

Did she really not recognize me? I could only nod. A room, yes.

'You're in luck again. You didn't reserve ahead, but we have something available with a beautiful view of town. It will do nicely for a visitor. Name?'

I stared at her. I knew she would not have thought of me during my absence, I knew it must be quite a shock, me being here now, but how, seeing me, could she not know me?

'Name, madam?' she said again.

'*Vera*. Marie, it's *Vera*.'

She looked at me with open, earnest eyes. My name meant nothing to her. 'May I ask you to sign our guest registry, Vera?' She gestured to a thick leather-bound volume open on the desk. I read the names written there, and I recognized many. They had been children when I left. Now they had signed the book in pairs before passing through the honeymoon suite. Di's son. Marie's stepdaughter. Ana's eldest, Teresa. I inscribed my name in the blank row at the bottom.

'I think you'll find your stay with us very restful. I imagine you'll not have seen any place quite so beautiful before.'

'It does seem lovely,' I found myself saying.

She handed me a brass key. 'Top of the stairs. Welcome, Vera. We're so happy you're here.'

Elsewhere had aged me. This was what I tried to tell myself that night as I settled into my room. My skin had turned thin and papery. Fine creases spread from the corners of my eyes. Like the ramparts that held up the promenade, like the cliff faces, I was weathered by the salt wind, the cold raw months, the sharp heat of the season. Such effects would be unfamiliar and illegible to the people here, where the damp air kept them supple and preserved. Maybe I appeared more altered to them than I could comprehend. Besides, when I went into the bathroom, I saw I looked dreadful from my journey, hair wild, face smudged with dirt. I undressed and ran a bath, an unpleasant one: I had forgotten that the water here never got hot; it was the same temperature as everything else, the air, the clouds.

I left my room only once that night, for supper in the empty dining room. I was served by a boy who looked to be in his twenties. He was shy with me. His hands shook when he set down my meal. The hands were glossy and stiff with scars; he was the boy who had reached into the ashes when his mother went. He gave no indication of recognizing me, but he would have been a teenager when I fled, preoccupied with his own life, so there was no reason to be alarmed that he didn't know me. I ordered the pork stew with noodles, but it didn't taste as I remembered. The meat was tough and gamey. I could detect in it the animal's distress when it was killed. I spat gristle into my napkin; discreetly, I thought, though the boy caught me doing this, and looked at me with pity. The gravy was crude and thin. It left a taste in my mouth of turned milk, and in the night I awoke and was sick into the toilet.

In the morning I did my best to make myself more familiar. To all of them, but most of all I readied myself for Iris and Peter. I wove my hair into a single braid down my back. I wore the only dress I had brought because it reminded me of the dress I had worn to Iris's birthday party all those years ago. It was foolish to expect that she would still love the pretty things that had so moved her as a girl of five, but that was the only Iris I knew, the only one for whom I could prepare. I sat for breakfast in the dining room, served this time by a girl whose white pin said LETTIE. I ordered baked eggs and greens and they arrived topped with the crumbly white cheese I had not tasted since I left. I could smell its funk, a smell of goat hides in the rain. I took a bite and gagged, I could do nothing to control my response, and I felt again the doubled nature of return: How I had missed this taste, yearned for it, and how foul it was to me now, even as I shut my eyes and wished it tasted to me now as it had tasted to me then, and I knew that later I would be sick again.

After breakfast I went out. It was a dreary day, gray as always, and I walked the downtown streets. On the corner of Hauptstrasse and Bergstrasse I saw Di's husband picking at his teeth under the awning of the bakery. Inside the bakery Lu sat across from June at a table, each of them eating a seeded roll. When June glanced up and spotted me through the window, she gripped Lu's hand and mouthed, '*Look.*'

On the residential streets I saw mothers on porches swaying with babies in their arms, and they waved at me eagerly, warily, as I passed. I walked to Peter's childhood home and there was his mother, white-haired, sitting on a low stool in her garden, yanking up weeds and shaking the soil from their roots. She stared at me as if I were a forest animal she would never have expected to see here, walking down the town streets. At Feldpark, small children skipped in my wake chanting, 'Hello, Vera! Vera, hello!' I wandered to the peripheries where the childless, solitary women lived. They pressed their faces to their windows. No one knew me.

I wanted to stand in front of the fountain in Feldpark and shout 'It's me! Vera! I'm Peter's wife and Iris's mother. I ran away and now I have come back.' But I sensed that I must not do this, that they would not, could not, believe me, that I had become unknowable to them the moment I passed out of the town. If I had come back to them sooner by a year, a decade, if after a single night elsewhere I had hurried straight home, it would not have mattered: I was not supposed to be here, and so I could not be here. I had come from elsewhere, so I could not be one of them. I had the feeling that I was coming to know a side of the affliction that could only be seen from the outside.

I went to the grove. Three women gathered fruit there. I couldn't identify two of them, but I knew the third must be Teresa. She looked just like Ana. The same thickness to her hair, the height and poise, and that look in her eyes, a glassy film of control over a roiling nature. She wore a burgundy blouse unbuttoned to reveal her elegant neck, around which hung a silver chain with a crystal pendant; this, too, had once been mine, long ago. The women were chattering away, but when they saw me they hushed. It was Teresa who approached me.

'Want to try?' She reached into her basket and held out a fruit.

'*Teresa!*' one of the women scolded.

'She's not allowed,' said the other, nervously.

'Oh, *relax*,' Teresa said, and rolled her eyes at them. She was the spitting image of Ana when she did that. She looked back at me with a sly smile. 'Most of us split them open and suck out the flesh, but I like the skin.'

'Like mother like daughter.'

'Pardon?' She looked at me curiously.

I had erred. Teresa didn't know me and couldn't understand how I would know her mother's preferences. 'I've met Ana. We spoke this morning,' I said. A lie, but one which I hoped would assuage her.

Teresa glanced back at her friends, who shook their heads. She returned her gaze to me, squinting as if trying to make out something within me. 'Who's Ana?'

So she had gone. All that time elsewhere, when the thought of her back here, enduring while I had failed to, had provided such unexpected comfort, Ana had been gone. When had it happened? I thought of the two of us in this grove years ago, on my last day in town, and how Ana had seemed to sense what was happening to me. Had she recognized it in me because it was in her, too? Maybe that was what she had been trying to tell me that day, only I had been too consumed with myself to understand. And I wondered if Ana's fate had hinged upon mine more than I had ever allowed myself to see. Maybe she had understood this all along, the danger of a pairing such as ours; maybe with everything she had done to me, severing our friendship, every cruelty, the countless petty torments by which she pushed me away, she had been trying, the only way she knew how, to save us both.

When I didn't reply, Teresa and her friends looked at one another, bemused. I held the fruit uncertainly in my hand. Teresa must have taken it from the ground, because the skin was caked with dirt.

'You just *bite*,' she said. The other women suppressed giggles, and I knew they were thinking what pathetic, clueless creatures life elsewhere made of people, because once I would have thought this, too.

I held the fruit to my mouth and did as she said. I tasted the dirt, the bitter skin, and then the fruit spilled into my mouth. I swallowed it down too quickly to crack the tiny white seeds against my teeth, for the pulp in my mouth was nothing like I remembered; it tasted only rancid. I forced a smile. 'Delicious.'

Teresa lifted the rest of the fruit from my hand. 'I bet you've never tasted anything quite so sweet.' She raised the fruit to her mouth and bit.

It was afternoon by the time I made my way back to Hauptstrasse, and the streets were crowded. They were crowded for me, and I passed people I had never not known and they stared at me because I was a stranger to them. Liese, stepping out of the sporting goods store beside a boy who towered over her, her son, that same colicky baby she had once squeezed too hard. Rufina licking a mint ice cream on the sidewalk outside the ice cream parlor. Ana's youngest brother sitting beside his wife on a bench while she nursed their baby, leaning in to kiss his wife on the mouth, then fetching a glass flask of water from a bag at his feet and offering it to her. I never saw this kind of tender care elsewhere. They did not exalt mothers as we did here. But then, nor did they sacrifice them.

I was nearing the end of Hauptstrasse where Peter's dental practice had been. Though I was desperate to see him, I dreaded learning what had become of him, and most of all I dreaded the moment when I would look into his eyes and he would look back at me, unknowing.

The practice was still there, the door propped open with a wedge of wood to let in the damp air. I stepped inside. The door to the examination room was shut. I could hear a drill whirring. I sat on one of the hard-backed chairs in the waiting room, and after some time a patient came out of the examination room. The sight of me flustered her, she muttered 'hello' and hurried out, and some minutes later, he emerged, my Peter, his face still smooth and youthful, eyes bright and sharp as ever. How badly I wanted to run to him, to wrap my arms around him and bury my face in his chest and hold him and hold him, but I knew I could not do this.

'Vera,' he whispered.

Could it be?

'You're the talk of the town,' he continued. 'I was hoping I'd get to see you soon, but I didn't expect it to be here in my office. What seems to be the trouble?'

I was no one to him. I wanted to sink to the floor, but I forced myself to remain as I was.

'Toothache?' he asked helpfully.

How else to explain my presence in his office? I nodded, brought my hand to my jaw.

'I have patients back-to-back today, but I can squeeze you in tomorrow. Two?'

'Two,' I repeated.

He had noticed my distress, and he set a hand comfortingly on my shoulder. 'I don't know what dental care you've experienced elsewhere, but you have nothing to fear here. It's quite painless.'

I went out from the office in a daze. I stood on the sidewalk, not knowing where to go or what to do next. As I stood there, I became aware of music, not the muted attempts of children through parlor windows, but something nearer, traveling on the air. I followed the sound around the building to the alley out back, and there, book bag in the grass, bare feet in the mud, all skinny legs and cutoffs, bowing at a viola as if besieged from every side, was Iris.

I kept myself pressed against the wall of the building. She played with the instinct I had always desired but never found within myself. I watched her like she was a star arcing across the night sky, an object of power and beauty in the face of which I could do nothing but bear witness. I closed my eyes and let her playing fill me. If this was all I got, then it was enough, it was everything. I would carry it inside me to the end.

The music stopped and I opened my eyes. Iris let her instrument drop to her side, dangled it by its neck, swished it through the brush as if it were a thing of no value.

'Hey,' she said casually, though I could sense the ardor in her.

'That was wonderful,' I said.

She shrugged. 'It was whatever.'

'Your mother must love to hear you play.' It was too forward, but I couldn't help it. I needed to know.

'What mother?'

Her words were a relief, and they gutted me. 'Forgive me. I'm sorry.'

Mr. Phillips was right, she did look like me, though her eyes flashed as mine never had, like she was a different, more ferocious girl looking out from a face that had once been mine. How could she not see how alike we looked? How could everyone not see it, the resemblance between a mother and her daughter? She wore her silver pin speared into the thickest part of her braid.

'That's so pretty,' I said, pointing to it.

She let out the slightest smile. 'Thanks. Anyway, I should get back to this.' She raised her viola. She was so exactly a teenager, desirous and determined to conceal that desire beneath a veil of nonchalance.

'Of course.' I turned to go. When I reached the sidewalk, I glanced back at her. She was touching her fingers to the pin in her braid.

Again that night I ate dinner early and alone in the dining room at the Alpina, meat pie and salad, the greens swimming in a sour dressing, and again I was sick. I wanted, needed, to cry, but I couldn't release the wails that pressed at my throat because I was surveilled. I heard people coming and going in the corridor all night, though mine was the only occupied room.

Nothing had befallen Iris and Peter. They were perfectly well, and they were so beautiful, and I loved them so much, and they did not know me.

The townspeople were so interested in me. At the bakery, in the forest, in Feldpark, they pressed near, eager to observe me and to catch my attention. Always, a sense of motion at the edges of my vision, figures darting at the periphery, a whole society adjusting itself around me. They were so full of questions. Had I enjoyed my breakfast? Was I having a wonderful visit? Didn't I find the town extraordinarily beautiful? Nobody asked where I had come from or why I was here. They wanted only to hear what I thought of them. To their questions I gave the answers I knew they wanted me to provide: *Yes, it is lovely. It is beautiful. I have never seen any place like it. There is nothing more to need.*

My bangle. My silver chain with the crystal pendant. My brown coat. My scarf with the gold embroidery. Everywhere, scattered among the girls and women of the town, I saw the remains of my own possessions.

I returned to the dental office for my appointment. Peter was waiting for me. He wore his white coat over gray slacks, the same black loafers he'd had when I left, or a new pair of the same. There were pale pink stains on the coat. I used to wait for the sun to break through, then soak his coat in bleach and hang it to dry on the line, but he had no one to do this for him now. I touched my hand to my jaw in what I hoped was a convincing simulation of pain. He ushered me down the hall to the examination room, gestured at the beige chair at its center. I had sat in this chair as a girl while Peter's father filled my cavities. I had sat in it the first time Peter touched me, and with Iris in my lap, singing to calm her so that Peter could examine her baby teeth. I must have sat in this chair in my own mother's lap once. Peter worked the pedals and I stayed still as the chair reclined until I lay supine.

'Open, please.'

I stretched my jaw wide, offering my mouth to him. I thought surely he would know me by these teeth, this throat. He took up his implements and reached into my mouth. He didn't wear gloves. The fine hairs on the tops of his hands brushed against my lips.

'Hmm.' He retracted his hands and furrowed his brow.

'Yes?' I said hopefully.

'I've just never seen—I don't know what I expected.' He laughed briefly to himself. 'Your teeth have a beautiful structure. Lie back again, please.'

I did as he asked.

'Ah, yes, I see the trouble.' He swiveled his chair away from me, and from a small table he picked up a needle, inserted it in a small glass vial and drew up a yellow liquid. 'A numbing agent,' he explained. 'Now lie still.'

I felt the needle pierce my gum, the liquid trickle down onto the back of my tongue, the taste of bitterness itself.

'This won't hurt,' he said. He lifted the drill from the table and brought it whirring into my mouth.

I couldn't eat that evening. All night I writhed in pain. When I touched my tongue to the tooth Peter had drilled the pain turned blinding, yet I couldn't stop pressing it, couldn't leave alone the hole he had made there.

I wanted only to be near Iris and Peter, to have them any way I could. I was discreet. I learned the rhythms of their days and tried to orchestrate run-ins. This turned out to be easy. Like nearly everyone in town, they were also seeking me out. We moved in revolutions around one another. In this way, I learned Iris. When she walked on Hinter der Wald, she liked to brush a hand against the ferns that grew along the sidewalk and wipe the dew in her hair. She bought a small bag of chips at the grocery every day after school and ate them before she practiced her viola; when the bag was empty, she reached a hand inside, swiped her fingertips against the foil and licked the salt off of them. She had a little signature of tucking a flower stem in the back pocket of her cutoffs so the petals poked out.

I wanted to pluck her from this place, take her kicking and screaming, whatever was required, and I wanted never to leave. I wanted to stay here with her forever.

I said that nearly everyone in town sought me out, but there were exceptions. The solitary women kept away. I never saw them on the town's commercial streets or in Feldpark. I suppose it was their lack of interest in me that drew me to them. One evening when the clouds came out and everyone else was inside and I would not be seen, I went to the edge of the forest, where the women lived in houses spread far apart from one another. They had not retreated indoors. They were out and about, moving through the clouds like ghosts. The women I remembered were still here. On one porch, a woman rocked on a swing, brought a cigarette to her lips and exhaled smoke, then pitched the spent stub into the forest without a care where it landed. Farther along, a woman stood at the edge of her yard tossing seeds to the earth. Up ahead of me on the path, a younger woman pushed a wheelbarrow piled high with dirt toward the last house. When she reached it, she carted her load around to the backyard and dumped it onto a pile of earth nearly as tall as the house. She must have sensed me behind her, because she turned, and through the veil of clouds I saw her: her hair flowing loose to her waist, her sharp widow's peak, and her eyes, which fixed on me with unmistakable warning.

One afternoon Iris was licking the salt from her fingertips when I came around, and she stuffed her hands down at her sides. I told her I used to love to do the same thing. She worked to suppress a smile.

'Best part,' she said.

'I used to buy a bag before my shifts at my father's shop. He owned a photography shop. We had a darkroom. We developed all the film for everyone in our town.'

'We don't have a photo shop here. My father says we used to.'

'Is that right? Who owned it?'

'Dunno.'

'Maybe I'll ask someone. I wonder what they'll say.'

She shrugged.

From the forest behind her came a rustling. Out of instinct I grabbed her hand, bracing for a feral goat to come squealing from the shadows. But it was just Teresa, her mouth smeared red from skinfruit. She eyed us furtively, then hurried on her way.

'Practically begging for it,' Iris scoffed when she was gone. She released her hand from mine. 'You should get back to the Alpina before the clouds come. We don't want you getting lost.'

One afternoon, I asked Iris if she was sad not to have a mother.

'It's not like that here,' she said.

'Tell me what it's like.'

She shook her head. 'I'm sorry. You seem like a really nice lady, but I don't think you'd get it.'

'How old were you?'

'Five.'

'But you don't remember her?'

'Of course I remember her,' she snapped.

'What did she look like?'

She rolled her eyes, as if it really was ridiculous, the things people from elsewhere needed explained. 'She looked like my mother.'

. . .

I returned to Peter's office.

'It hurts,' I said, massaging my cheek, and this time it was true. My jaw throbbed relentlessly.

I sat in the beige chair and offered my mouth to him.

'It's healing nicely,' he said.

'Please. The pain. You have to help me.'

He cradled my cheek in his hand. He leaned over me, the bright dentist's light shining behind his head. 'I know it hurts now, but I promise your jaw will acclimate. Your teeth must be unaccustomed to the snap of our fresh food here. It will take time. I hope you're planning to stay.' As he spoke, his fingertips moved absently against my cheek. I would know those notes anywhere. He was playing the cello part from the piece we had played at our last recital, and I thought some part of him must remember that he had done this before, playing the notes against the cheek of the woman who had been his wife, and maybe if I said or did just the right thing I could bring that part of him to the surface, and he would know me.

'Come to my room at the Alpina tonight,' I said.

His hand stilled. I had shocked him.

'I'm sorry,' I muttered. 'I'm not used to how it is here, like you said. I misunderstood.'

He shook his head. 'You didn't.'

Night after night he came to me. In a bed at the Alpina, beside a window that overlooked all the world Peter had ever known, we made love for hours. What did Peter make of the way I knew just how to touch him, the way he knew just how to touch me, the pleasure we wrested from one another? Did he think it was our being unknown to one another that allowed such strangeness to seep into our lovemaking? Could he really not see it was intimacy, which his body remembered even though his mind did not, that unearthed this strangeness? He thrust his fingers inside me and they emerged coated in a white film like the vernix on a newborn's skin. He plunged one of the fingers into my mouth and I tasted myself. He pressed the finger to my sore tooth as I came, pain and pleasure impossible to sort.

Maybe Peter and Iris didn't need to remember me for me to have them again. Maybe it was better like this. They could love the stranger Vera, and she could stitch herself into their lives. I could become Peter's wife and Iris's mother anew. Before long, I might barely remember the first life we had shared, and it wouldn't matter that Iris didn't know I had rocked her through the nights as a baby, that Peter didn't know I had tasted his blood as a girl of twenty, that neither of them knew they had burned my image. I would be two women in the beginning, the first Vera swallowed by the second and living in the darkness inside her, but the longer it went on the less it would matter that we were two, the clearer it would become that we were also one.

The next morning when I came down to the dining room for breakfast, Lettie wasn't there. I went to check with Marie at the front desk, but there, too, I found no one. I went out onto Hauptstrasse, but the usually bustling morning sidewalks were empty and the clouds hung over the cobbles undisturbed. It wasn't until I went to the residential backstreets and saw the people milling about, and beginning to walk in one direction, that I understood. I joined the crowd, walking among people who once I would not even have thought of as people, but simply as *us*. A woman next to me held her baby close to her chest and swayed. She whispered to her husband, 'They're saying it's Teresa.'

I had not felt it. I had not sensed our diminishment as I used to on these mornings. I had bathed and dressed without the slightest alteration to my perceptions. I should have seen it then. I thought I was one of them, only they couldn't remember, they were under the misapprehension that I was a stranger from elsewhere. I should have seen then that it was I who was mistaken, but still I did not see it.

I walked among them, flowed with them down the streets. People nodded at me, shy but approving. It was a solemn occasion, but they were happy I had joined them, that I should see them on this day when they became most themselves. By the time I reached Teresa's house, the lawn was nearly full, and I found a space near the edge. But as people continued to arrive, I found myself pressed toward the center, packed in more and more tightly. All around me I heard the chatter, women discussing Teresa's indications, piecing her apart and tossing up signs. Teresa fed too often from the grove. She cried when she nursed, whether tears of bliss or sorrow they couldn't say. When she was a young girl she bit other girls, as if jealous already of something that was in them, or wasn't. A mother who had attended new mom group with Teresa attested that once, when Teresa's baby spit up, she had gotten some of the sour white liquid, her own curdled milk, on her fingers, and sneakily licked it off. She put necklaces on her tiny baby, blue beads on white string. Her love was too animal, or it was too frivolous. She had always been like this, or had undergone a sudden rupture. I wondered then if the affliction possessed any secret logic at all. It seemed to me that all that connected the mothers who went was that they were gone, and that everyone they had ever known had decided there was a reason for it, and a purpose far greater than the loss.

When the front door opened, the crowd hushed as if a great wind had died, and I watched Teresa's husband emerge, the small baby with the blue necklace in his arms. The father carried the baby to the porch swing and together they wailed and rocked as the mothers loaded wheelbarrows with Teresa's possessions, and as the men combed through the house for her image. When the work was complete, the fire was lit and the pile burned, and as it burned I closed my eyes and tried to speak to Teresa. *Your mother's name was Ana. She ate the earth like you and she was cruel, and she loved you. She named you years before you were born.*

That night I joined the assembly at Feldpark for the recital. I listened to the kinders send their soft ardent voices into the night, saw the firsts' recorders glow like long tongues in the darkness. The years filed onto and off of the stage until at last it was time for the uppers. It was a difficult piece, a six-note motif appearing infrequently at first, but recurring with ever-greater insistence as the piece progressed, until it consisted of nothing but return, and the music sealed itself shut, a locked chamber. Iris bowed with her eyes clenched shut. She was stunning, she was brutal, and when she finished she opened her eyes as if surfacing from the sea.

Later that night, when Peter came to the Alpina, it seemed to me that we had sex as we had long ago, fueled by the witness we had born to Iris, to the absolute, sacred perfection of her.

The next afternoon, Iris wore the silver necklace with the crystal pendant.

'Is that new?' I asked.

'Just found it at the Op Shop. Isn't it great?'

Soon Iris would put on this necklace and think only how much it suited her. And would some other woman, herself now just a young girl, clasp it around her neck someday? Tears filled my eyes.

'You're upset about yesterday,' she said.

I nodded.

'Mr. Phillips gets sad like that sometimes.'

'I keep thinking of her daughter.'

'Her daughter will be fine.'

'But aren't you afraid it might happen to you? You won't be a child much longer.'

For the first time, when she looked at me I saw in her expression no eagerness to please me or to win my approval. And I sensed in that moment that I had already begun to lose her. Yet how I clung to it, this exchange which, viewed from a certain angle, was so ordinary, nothing but a daughter bristling at her mother, and beginning to pull away.

'I'm not a child now.'

Iris must have told others about my reaction to Teresa's going, the judgment I couldn't help but express. Or perhaps it was simply evident, because the next day when I walked around town, watching the women come and go from the Op Shop, I sensed a change in the way they looked at me. There was something at once wounded and affronted in how they eyed me now, as if their fascination had begun to turn over into something else.

'I came here from the coast,' I told Iris the next afternoon.

'I didn't ask where you came from.'

'Still. You can't imagine the sea.'

'We have the Graubach,' she countered.

'The sea is nothing like the Graubach.'

'I know it's bigger.' She rolled her eyes. 'And saltier.'

I reached into my satchel and withdrew a photograph from my folio. 'I want you to have this.' I pressed the picture into her hands and she studied it a moment: the promenade, the booths, the sea beyond, the cliffs and the spray as the water dashed itself against them.

'I should burn this. I should throw it in the Graubach.'

But as I left, I saw her tuck it into her viola case.

When the clouds gathered that evening, I went once more to the edge of town. The woman who pitched burning embers into the trees. The woman who tossed seeds to the earth. The woman with the wheelbarrow was depositing a load of soil onto her pile when I arrived at her house. When she had finished, she laid her shovel in the wheelbarrow and set out again, into the forest. I followed her. She walked no regular path, but her route was worn smooth by her own comings and goings. I kept my distance, wary of being seen. We moved through dense growth, climbing steeply upward all the while, and I was thoroughly disoriented when I heard the sound of rushing water. She had come to a portion of the Graubach we never visited, high above town. She pushed the barrow up to the top of the embankment, removed the shovel, and began to dig. She must have been digging here for months, years. The embankment was half as high as farther downstream. She went about her work calmly and efficiently and she appeared never to tire. When her barrow was full she carted the earth away.

The next afternoon, I came upon Iris when she was practicing viola, but when she saw me approach, she stopped playing.

'Please,' I said. 'I love to hear you.'

She shrugged.

'Do you know in the city nearest to here, there's a cathedral? At eventide the bells ring. It's very beautiful.'

'I doubt I would find it beautiful.'

'Maybe someday you'll hear it and decide for yourself.'

She glared at me. 'I know where my father goes at night,' she said. 'I know you aren't what you pretend to be.'

In the beginning, the people here had pressed near to me. Now they kept away. In Feldpark, the benches to either side of mine remained unoccupied. When I walked the residential streets, children no longer followed in my wake chanting my name, and when a child too young to understand this sudden shift left their porch steps and ran to me, their mother threw down her weaving and chased after them. When I arrived at the grove, the mothers gathered their baskets without a word and departed. On my way back to town, I stumbled over up-turned stones, tripped over branches, snagged my skin on the thorns of skinfruit vines coiled along the path, traps laid for me alone.

The next afternoon I asked Iris to come for a walk with me, and grudgingly she complied. I led her down the streets of town to Hinter der Wald, to her own house, then around back to the yard.

She tossed her book bag in the dirt, leaned her viola case on top, crossed her arms. 'We're here why?'

'In the parlor there's a sofa with gold upholstery. The kitchen plates are white with blue edges. Your father keeps the tea in an old pretzel tin.'

I had her attention now.

'On your right elbow you have a scar from when you tried to walk across a fallen tree in the forest. You used to dab cinnamon behind your ears and pretend it was perfume.'

'My father tells you these things.'

'Iris, please. You know who I am.'

She reached out to me then. She took my braid in her hand, stroked her fingertips back and forth across the smooth plaits. Then she tossed it away like something dirty.

'I know what you would have us believe. But you look nothing like my mother. You look like a stranger.'

That night, Peter came to me at the Alpina for the last time. Did I know it then? It seems to me I must have, for I made love to him as I had made love to him on that other last night, so many years ago, with a desperate hope that through this act I might make myself into a woman who could remain here. I had no hairpin, but on that night I did what I had not dared to do before. I brought my mouth to his skin and with my teeth that Peter had tended, and drilled open, I pierced him. The blood welled and I licked it clean, and when he brought me to the edge and my mouth opened with pleasure, I hoped that he would see my teeth coated with his blood and he would finally know me, and he would be able to show the rest of them who I was, even as I knew by then that this would not happen, that there was nothing I could show them, nothing I could do or say to make them see.

In the morning when I looked out my window, I saw the people of the town waiting for me down below.

When I came out the front entrance of the Alpina, they were massed before me.

Marie came forward. 'You'll be checking out today. Lettie is upstairs packing your things.'

'Please don't make me go. I want to stay.'

Marie snorted. 'We know you *want* to stay.'

A moment later, Lettie appeared at my side and forced my bag
into my hands. The crowd began to move toward me as one. They
pressed against me. I tried to keep my feet fixed to the ground, but
they were too powerful, and I was compelled to walk, pushed along as
by a great wave. Down Hauptstrasse, past the Op Shop and the bakery and Peter's office and the school and the shop front that had once
been Rapid Ready. Onto Bergstrasse, to Feldpark and the statue of the
crying woman and the fields where Ana and I had played together as
girls. Past Eschen and Hinter der Wald and into the forest, through the
grove and then beyond it. Despite our numbers, we processed in near
silence, and I could hear the Graubach through the trees, the rush and
slip of water over rock. Soon we had reached it. We climbed over the
embankment and I stood at the river's edge and turned to face them.
Iris had made her way to the front. She stood inches away from me.

'Iris,' I begged. 'Please.' I threw myself upon her. I grasped at her
clothes, her braid, wrapped my arms around her neck, breathed her
skin. I wanted to cling to her until I was ripped from her, to refuse to
go, and to refuse, until there was nothing left of me. But my feet were
beginning to slip on the muddy bank. I knew what would happen,
and I could not let it, could not allow Iris to carry it, even if she might
never know what she had done.

I released my grip on her. I stepped back, and we stared at each
other.

'I love you,' I whispered.

For a moment she seemed to hear these words, maybe even to feel

214 • ALEXIS SCHAITKIN

them. But she quickly regained her composure. 'You will never understand us,' she said. 'Not if you live here a hundred years.'

Once again, I turned and ran from my child. I did not stop until I had reached the supply road and the town disappeared from view.

V

went back to Mr. Phillips.

'How nice to see you again. Please come in,' Judith said when she opened the door. Her displeasure at my return was evident, but she concealed it admirably, and I thought that Mr. Phillips must have selected her because she, like he, was a consummate professional. She led me to the parlor. 'Mr. Phillips will be along in a minute. He's just finishing with his bandages. Make yourself comfortable.' I sat in the same damask chair as before, and Judith returned shortly with the lacquer tray, the tea and shortbread, and laid these out without a word, then retreated to the kitchen. A few minutes later Mr. Phillips appeared in the parlor doorway. He was greatly altered from the last time I had seen him, though it had been only a few weeks. He walked with a cane, a simple black piece, and he made his way stiffly across the room. When he saw me opening my mouth to speak, he put up his hand and waved away my concern.

'A fall,' he said. 'Nothing, really. Only my skin is so thin now, like insect wings. It's slow to heal.' He lowered himself with great effort onto the sofa and busied himself with the spread laid out by Judith, pouring himself tea, swirling milk into the cup, using the silver tongs to drop in two sugar cubes, stirring them with a small silver spoon until they melted away. He took a sip, set the teacup down, folded his hands in his lap.

'Well then. How was your visit, Vera?'

'The stranger Ruth,' I said. 'She was my mother.'

He took a bite of shortbread, chewed it thoughtfully, nodded.

I saw us, Ruth and me, together in Rapid Ready, separated only by the worn counter. How she reached out her hand and let our fingertips brush as she paid for her film, and all I thought was that she was learning to be like us. She was right there. I had touched her. Yet I couldn't see it. I saw only a stranger. 'I drove her into the water.'

'Don't be so hard on yourself. You did just what you were supposed to do. Besides, you didn't spurn her completely. You kept the photograph, after all.'

'You remember her. I don't mean when she was out here. Before she left. I can't remember her, but you must.'

He didn't reply right away, and I thought he would claim that this was yet another subject about which he was obligated to be discreet. Then a smile fell over his face, vague and distant, as if at some private, tucked-away memory.

'She used to let you wear a little of her lipstick on supply days. You used to kiss your doll so she had lipstick, too.'

'Walina.' I thought of Iris, how I had done the same thing for her on supply days, and I wondered if maybe some part of me that I could not access did remember my mother. I thought maybe this one memory was enough, maybe it was all I needed, and for a moment I felt nothing but gratitude toward Mr. Phillips for giving it to me.

He took another sip of his milky, oversweet tea.

'You knew what would happen to me there. You knew they would think I was a stranger. You knew they would turn against me.'

'You can't say I didn't try to dissuade you from returning,' he replied evenly. He took another shortbread from the tray and snapped it between his front teeth.

'That's not true. You wanted me to go. You made me believe you were keeping something terrible from me about Iris. You tricked me.'

He shrugged. 'Every generation needs a stranger.'

I saw us then, a thread of mothers and daughters slipping through one another's grasp. We were the strangers. We fled so that our love for our daughters might not vanish from this earth and we returned to save them, but we couldn't save them, our return did nothing but show the town that a stranger could not be trusted, that elsewhere had nothing to offer them, reminding them, if they should ever begin to doubt it, of the beauty and necessity of their lives in that place. And we could do nothing but leave our daughters with some trace of ourselves and hope that maybe, someday, they would come find us.

'You help it to continue,' I said finally. 'You make it possible.'

'You flatter me. I'm just the supplier.'

'You could put a stop to it. If you didn't go back, if you didn't bring them what they need to survive, they would have to come down the mountain.'

'Is that what you would want?'

I fell silent. Mr. Phillips's lip curled with pleasure, for he could see it plainly: In spite of everything, I could not wish the town gone.

'Anyway, an irrelevant hypothetical,' he said, cuffing his sweater. 'They would never come down the mountain. They would find another way. Surely you must see now that it cannot be undone.'

I thought of the solitary women. Maybe someday the seeds the woman scattered would grow until they suffocated everything, the streets and the houses and the fields. Maybe a dry spell would come and when the woman threw her ember, it would finally catch and burn everything to ash. Maybe an unprecedented rainstorm would cause the river to rise and the embankment to collapse where the woman had dug away at it, and the town would wash away. But I didn't think so.

'Still, you enable it. You play your part.'

'And now you've played yours. Though I won't be playing mine much longer, I'm afraid.' He gestured at himself, his leg, his general frailty. 'My successor has been ready for some time now, but I must admit I've found it rather difficult to relinquish my post.' He chuckled. 'The older I get, I wonder. Does the town exist because we require it? I mean all of us out here, elsewhere.'

'That's a pretty notion.'

'But perhaps not wrong. Perhaps not wrong.' He drank the last of his tea, ate the final shortbread on the tray. 'So, Vera. What will you do now?'

The season has barely begun. The air is still raw, the ocean flat and gray. Not long ago I walked the promenade and watched snow fall into the sea. But the hotels held their fair last week, after which the girls came to me for lodging.

It's been nearly a decade since Miss Ben suffered her stroke and I took over the boardinghouse; I still visit her the first Sunday of every month at the home for the aged where she lives, an hour inland. All these hopeful girls, descending from the trains with their carefully tended hopes for their futures. I am Miss Vera to them, and they begrudge me my rules even as they love me. They love me without understanding that it is their own mothers they love, and who they are trying to touch through me.

When I first took over, the girls here were a few years older than

Iris, and then for a few seasons they were just about her age, and now they are much younger than her, or she is much older than them, if she still is at all.

For a long time after I returned to the coast, nothing mattered to me and I assumed nothing ever would again. But life goes on so long, and once more, the direction of mine has surprised me. I have known purpose and pleasure. I have, for stretches, been busy and nearly happy.

Recently, outside the season, I have begun teaching a photography class at a local community center. The center was established in response to the arrival, in towns and cities all along the coast, of refugees escaping a war in the city across the sea that I visited during my transient period after leaving the coast. When my students speak of their city to me, they always come back to the light, that famous, dazzling light, like no place else. They confess to an almost unbearable homesickness for it. It is a clear light that renders the landscape exquisitely sharp, making it possible to pick out details of distant hills that should be just a blur. This clarity cannot be fully explained by the city's low humidity or its topography; it is something of a mystery.

The war was brief only because it was too terrible to be sustained. A civil war, fought among farmers and shop owners, waged with kitchen knives and composed of the most intimate atrocities. When it began, everybody said how terrible it was that such a beautiful place should be destroyed, should destroy itself; terrible and incomprehensible, a war among the people of such a place, as if the city's beauty should have worked against such acts.

People used to speculate that the city's distinctive light was the result of the way its limestone buildings reflected the sun. But now many of those buildings are gone, rendered uninhabitable by the war and leveled shortly thereafter, and concrete construction rises in their place, and still, my students tell me, according to relatives who stayed behind and who they may never see again, the light, the city, are so beautiful. I have the sense that whatever is torn down and rebuilt there, the city will always be beautiful and terrible things will always happen there.

My students don't talk about the dark acts they witnessed or the dark acts I'm sure some of them committed. They don't have to. It is in their photographs. They can take a picture of the clock tower in the center of town, surf smashing the cliffs, the revelers on Wight Street. It doesn't matter. Every photograph is a photograph of their city. With each one they are trying to get back there, to the ghost city beyond this town and to their ghost selves.

My students, the girls at the boardinghouse . . . it seems to me that everyone has come from a place they will never move on from, a place they hate and love in equal measure, a place people elsewhere can never understand; they find me here, and I believe I am useful to them, though I know this place can only ever be a disappointment to them.

Sometimes I am able to go whole days without thinking of the town. I can almost convince myself I knew no life before this one. Then something will happen. Just recently, walking the backstreets at dawn to clear my mind, I saw an old woman emerge from her house in a lace-trimmed blouse and matching skirt, hair set in curls, heavy rouge on her cheeks, and the sight of her reminded me of something I couldn't touch or name. I pass a woman on the promenade with a baby in her arms, swaying, and I see us gathered on the lawn on those mornings, and a feeling comes over me that is nothing but the faded afterimage of what it felt like to be there, to be us. I hear music floating from an open window and suddenly I smell the dampness, feel it in my hair. I see ferns pushing up between cobblestones, spiderwebs sprouting from eaves, glistening with dew.

I imagine that when I die, if they cut me open they will find my bones overgrown with moss and vines, and in the cathedral of my rib cage they will find our town in all its detail, Hauptstrasse my spine, our house on Hinter der Wald, the Alpina and the Graubach and the grove. Maybe I have always carried this inside me: another elsewhere that is neither high above nor down below, but within. In this place we are all together and always have been, Ana and Teresa, Ruth and Iris and me, kept safe from the world and from ourselves, and in this place, at last, we have everything we need.

I will never leave the coast. I will wait for Iris until I am air.

Acknowledgments

My deep gratitude to my editor, Deb Futter, who completely understood this novel when it was still a mess and gave it the time it needed to clean itself up. I am so thankful for your kindness, your patience, and your brilliant notes. Thank you to the all-star team at Celadon, including Rachel Chou, Christine Mykityshyn, Anne Twomey, Randi Kramer, Jennifer Jackson, Jaime Noven, Anna Belle Hindenlang, Rebecca Ritchey, Heather Orlando-Jerabek, Audine Cross, Sandra Moore, and Erin Cahill. To Frances Sayers, Adriana Coada, Michelle McMillian, and Emily Walters in production, Shelly Perron for her terrific copyediting, and Callum Plews, whom I was fortunate enough to work with again on the production of the audiobook.

Thank you to my agent, Henry Dunow, for your steadfast support. I am so very lucky to have had you as my champion for nearly a decade. To Arielle Datz for everything you do for my books. A million thanks to Sylvie Rabineau and Lauren Szurgot for working to make my dreams come true.

To Greg Jackson, Clare Beams, and Ali Benjamin for your incisive and generous reads of various drafts of this novel. To Amanda Dennis, Eva Hagberg, Juhea Kim, Rachel Lyon, Kate McQuade, Dina Nayeri, and Keija Parssinen for your friendship and for reading the novel's early pages.

To Roberta Sweet for caring so tenderly for our newborn as I wrote, wrote, wrote to finish this book.

To my family for your love and support, and especially to my mother: Every day I see more clearly all that you have done for me, and do for me still.

To Emerson: I love you infinity plus one. Johanna: Welcome to the world, sweet child. We're so happy you're here.

Thank you to my husband, Mason, for being my first and wisest reader, for believing in me—and in this book—so completely, and for moving mountains to give me the time to finish it during a pandemic, with one small child at home and another on the way. Our partnership, and this family we have built together, are the great joys of my life.

About the Author

Alexis Schaitkin is the author of *Saint X*. Her short stories have been anthologized in *The Best American Short Stories* and *The Best American Nonrequired Reading*. She received her MFA in fiction from the University of Virginia, where she was a Henry Hoyns Fellow. She lives in Williamstown, Massachusetts, with her husband and their two children.